MATCHED AND MATED

INTERSTELLAR BRIDES® PROGRAM - BOOK 16

GRACE GOODWIN

GET A FREE BOOK!

Join my mailing list to be the first to know of new releases, free books, special prices and other author giveaways.

http://freescifiromance.com

INTERSTELLAR BRIDES® PROGRAM

YOUR mate is out there. Take the test today and discover your perfect match. Are you ready for a sexy alien mate (or two)?

VOLUNTEER NOW!

interstellarbridesprogram.com

1

*M*iranda Doyle, Xalia City, Southern Continent, Planet Trion

GENTLE FINGERS MADE their way through my long dark hair as Brax tamed it into a long braid. I knelt on the bed and closed my eyes, reveling in the feel of his attention. Even this non-erotic task was arousing in its simplicity. I felt like the star in a movie I'd seen before transporting here—a movie where the hero braided his lover's hair, then took her into a special room filled with toys.

Yes. This was exactly like that. For I had no doubt that as soon as Brax was finished, he would *play* with me for *hours.*

I'd been waiting for this night, for his return from duty, for weeks. Doctor Valck Brax was a sought after male on Trion. Everyone in the city knew he was a brilliant doctor and Councilor Roark's most trusted advisor. What many didn't know was that Brax was also regularly sent on dangerous missions he could tell me nothing about.

Despite his frequent absences from the city, I wasn't the

only one who wanted a piece of the gorgeous male. With his dark hair, darker eyes and a smile that promised wicked, wanton pleasure, he was all mine... at least for a day or two. Then he would, once again, be called to duty, don his uniform and return to being a soldier-spy as well as a doctor. When he was naked, he was mine. Clothed... he was a Trion warrior with duties and allegiance to his councilor.

His fingers tugged, then rubbed the tension from my temples. I wanted to melt into a puddle and beg him to pet me for hours, but we were on borrowed time. I didn't want to waste a single moment of it. But the tension gave me away. I couldn't stop thinking about the past. My past.

I'd come across the universe to this strange planet because there was nothing left for me on Earth. I had an ex-husband and putting several light years between us had been fine by me. He'd been all missionary, all the time, and had told me the devil was inside me for needing something more, for even thinking of it. He'd practically run to the shower after every time we had sex. I often wondered that he hadn't stubbed his toe in the dark—since we'd never done it once with the lights on. He'd made me believe there was something wrong with me. That I was somehow twisted. Perverted. Filthy, even. Now, I knew there had been something wrong with *him*.

Divorce had been an easy decision. Coming here to Trion with Natalie and baby Noah had been even easier. I'd wanted something more then, but I hadn't known what it was. Finally, tonight, after months with Brax, I *knew*. I wanted what Natalie had. I wanted a mate like her Roark. I wanted a baby of my own. Family. Safety. Protection.

I needed to *belong*.

When I'd first arrived, taking care of Noah and watching Natalie's back had been enough. But Noah was two now—

not a baby anymore. And I'd begun to heal. I had always wanted a husband, but after the divorce I knew I wasn't ready for another.

I'd come out here, to a new planet, to find *me*.

I had questions that needed answers. Like why I'd never found basic vanilla sex with my ex to be arousing. Why he'd made me feel broken and dirty for wanting things he couldn't understand. That I couldn't understand. I didn't know what to think. Or feel. Or want.

Until Brax. Until he opened my eyes to what I desired. What I needed. Craved.

A tug to my hair.

Restraints.

The sharp sting of a spanking on my ass.

The sharp thrust of a huge cock filling me from behind when I was tied down and helpless.

The newfound confidence I'd discovered within myself was something Brax had given me over the last few months. But tonight would either be a new beginning for us, or an ending. The *friends with benefits* arrangement we'd had since the beginning wasn't enough for me anymore. A wild few days when he was in town and off-duty couldn't satisfy me any longer. Oh, he'd give me orgasms and make me a sweaty heap, but I wanted more than sex with him.

I was finally whole, ready to give my heart away—and Brax was more than halfway to claiming it already.

I wanted everything Natalie had, everything I'd followed her to Trion to have for myself. I loved looking after Noah, and his new little sister, but seeing Natalie give birth to a second child—the little baby girl now only days old—made me yearn for the first time in years. My ovaries practically exploded just holding her.

But Brax didn't want babies. He didn't want a mate. He

didn't want anything more than a fun time. I wasn't mad. I hadn't wanted more either... until I did. And that wasn't his fault.

"You are quiet tonight, Miranda." Brax tied something around the end of my braid to secure it and lowered his lips to my bare shoulder. The soft, heated touch was like the brush of fire against my skin.

"I'm sorry, Master." In this room, his bedroom, I never used his name. I didn't have permission. When we were together, he was my master in every way, and I'd come to learn that with my surrender came amazing pleasure.

He moved in closer, and I gasped as his bare chest came to rest against my back. I wore next to nothing, sexy layers of gossamer silk that would not impede his hands, his mouth, or his cock from finding any part of me he desired. It was so pretty, decadent even, a shimmering fabric like translucent liquid opals. I'd never seen anything like it on Earth, and I'd spent two week's wages from my job at the youth education center to wear it for Brax tonight.

"Do you wish to share what troubles you?" His hands rested on my waist, and I could feel the patience in him. Heard it in the soft tone of his voice. He would wait if I wished. Would listen. But that wasn't what I needed from him, for I already knew the answer. We'd agreed to no strings and that's what we'd done all this time. A wild few days and then he walked away. It had been hot, easy and simple.

Until it wasn't. Not in my mind... and crap, not in my heart. I wouldn't ruin this time with him by telling him I wanted more, wanted to change the rules of our arrangement. It wasn't fair to him, especially since I knew his answer. He was content as it was. And that was why I remained silent. I didn't *want* his answer, didn't want to hear him tell me again about his duty to his people. His loyalty to Roark. I didn't need a list of the reasons he wasn't ready to take a mate. The reasons he *couldn't* take a mate. I already *knew* exactly what he would say.

No. I needed to forget—and feel. And if this was the last time, so be it.

"No, Master."

"Then tell me what you need."

The soft murmur of his voice settled within me, to the very heart of what made me... well, me. That soft request opened doors in my mind that no one else had ever opened. That, before Brax, I'd been too terrified to even peek through. But I understood now. I needed to surrender. I needed to feel safe and give someone else control. I needed to trust him to take care of me. That need drove me to kneel, to call him *master,* to give him anything he wanted because I trusted him to take care of me. I'd been afraid my entire life. With Brax, I obeyed... and I was free. While I might be submitting, he would give me my every desire. And right now, there was only one thing I wanted. I *needed.*

"You."

The word was barely more than a sigh, and true in ways he couldn't possibly understand. I'd approached him, after all. I'd arrived on Trion with Natalie and Noah almost two years ago. Then, I hadn't been ready. But six months ago, I'd gone to Brax and offered my body, asked him to make love to me. He'd refused, at first. He hadn't laughed at the request or shamed me, thank god. He'd studied me in that intense way of his, then asked me to explain my need to be fucked. By him. A stranger.

Trion was different. God, sooo unbelievably different. Males on Trion were so unlike Earth men, especially my ex. My ex would have scoffed and called me a slut. But Brax had sensed there was an underlying reason for my request, that I wasn't asking simply because I wanted to get off or had a dark demon within me.

And so I'd taken the biggest risk of my life and told him the truth. I told him about my ex, my past, how I didn't know what my body truly needed, but that I needed... *something.* I had admitted that I had been watching the females on Trion for months. Admiring them with their adornments and shimmering clothing. They were shameless. Bold. They submitted to their mates willingly and with a peacefulness that I envied. They were content. Blissfully, brazenly sensual. Trion females didn't have to ask for sex. They *exuded* it.

At that time, I hadn't exuded anything except lingering doubts from my bad marriage. And that was what Brax had seen. Then questioned with a relentless intensity I'd come to adore. As ruthless as he'd been with his questions about my past, he'd been equally merciless in his demands that I overcome it.

Having a doctor for a lover had certain benefits. He'd taken care of birth control with one injection, bent me over the table, and ordered me not to move while he *examined* me. More like, touched me everywhere—and I mean everywhere—and found out what made me burn.

Holy fuck, no wonder Trion males were so... hot. They took, but gave so thoroughly in return because—hello!—I found out I loved to be bent over and worked until I was a sweaty, sated mess. I loved knowing my body aroused him, that he enjoyed seeing me naked. Loved me *being* naked, not allowing my clothes to remain on for long when we were together.

And now, he used the knowledge he'd gained about me, running his palm up and down my spine, leaning me forward. I went where he wished, bending, then dropping into a kneeling position on my hands and knees as he remained behind me, caressing the globes of my bottom. He pulled them apart, looked his fill. "You have a beautiful pussy."

Knowing he could see me so thoroughly didn't shame me any longer; it made me hot. Made me wet. I shuddered, wishing he would slide his fingers inside my slick heat, touch my clit. Lick me. Nibble. Anything. The waiting was torture, and I whimpered.

His hand landed on my ass with a loud smack, making my breasts swing beneath me. Another. The sting traveled through my body and went straight to my core. "I gave you a compliment. What do you say?"

I hissed out a breath, felt the heat spread. "Thank you, Master."

Appeased, he leaned down and pressed his lips to the area I knew would be turning pink. "Your gown is beautiful, Miranda. Did you wear this for me?"

"Yes, Master." God, did I ever. I wanted him to lose his mind. Shove me down and fuck me until I couldn't see straight. I wanted him to take one look at me and decide he needed a mate after all. But I should have known better. Brax had *never* lost control. Not once.

"I have a gift for you as well." The way he said the words made them feel like sex inside my head. Being with him was the gift I gave myself once a month when he returned from the latest dangerous, secret mission he always seemed to be on. He might be a doctor, but he still served, and in a way more dangerous than others stationed in the capital city of Xalia. Those missions were the reason he'd told me he could not take a mate. The reason he'd insisted this *thing* between us was only temporary, a casual arrangement between friends.

At first he'd focused on breaking every barrier my ex had placed in my mind. He'd touched me places I'd never been touched. Forced me to touch myself. Touch him. He'd pushed every boundary I had until I'd broken. Once he'd turned me into a blatant sexual creature, our relationship had changed. Now we both fulfilled a need in the other. A physical need.

Now we were fuck buddies. A booty call. *Friends with benefits.*

I didn't want to be his friend. Not anymore. I wanted to be *his.* I was ready to belong again. Have someone of my own. I was ready to give my heart away, but I didn't want to make a mistake. Not this time. I would take what Brax offered me tonight because the *benefits* felt so damned good, and I'd deal with the rest of my life later.

"Thank you, Master."

He chuckled and I closed my eyes in pleasure. It was rare that I could make him laugh. "Don't you want to know what I bought for you before you thank me?"

I did. But I remained silent, didn't look over my shoulder to see what it might be. Until I felt his fingers slide between my legs to find my clit. Only then did my head come up. I hissed as something hard clamped down on that sensitive bit of flesh, and I moaned with shock, and a nip of pain. But within seconds, the pain transformed to pleasure, and I panted. "Thank you, Master."

His hand caressed my back once more, moving in soothing motions as I adjusted to the intense pressure on my clit. "I have two more, Miranda. Sit up and present your breasts to me."

I leaned back on my heels and returned to my original

kneeling position. When he moved around in front of me, he looked down between my parted thighs, saw the jewel dangling down from my pussy. Yes, Trion males loved to decorate their females. To adorn them and make them even more beautiful. Even more aroused.

I watched as he plucked and tugged at a nipple until the tip was hard, then placed a jeweled clamp on it. The sting was immediate, but my entire body shuddered with pleasure as he moved on to the other. I needed this, the bite, the pain, the shock that made my pussy practically weep.

I glanced down, saw the sharp clamps had green gems dangling from them. With each shuddering breath, they swayed. I felt beautiful. Special. I felt like I was the center of his world. I wanted everything he could give me... and more.

I wasn't sure what the *more* that I needed was yet, but I knew it was there within me, like an itch in my mind. No matter how many times Brax made me come, there was something else I required, a *yearning* I'd felt almost every day of my life. But the strange emptiness was buried so deep inside me that I couldn't hope to name it. That empty place ached all the time, like my soul had been bruised and never recovered.

At first, I'd ignored the painful loneliness and written the darkness off as teenage angst. Later, when I married, I'd begun to think that maybe the feeling was a permanent side-effect of my cold, rigid ex. But now, I wasn't sure. He'd made me feel like there was something wrong with me, like I was a deviant. A freak.

That's what I'd believed, until Brax broke me free of my sexual prison. And if my ex looked at me now? Naked except for some frothy fabric, dripping wet and desperate for an alien who'd put clamps on my clit and nipples, he wouldn't recognize me. And yet, I wanted more. Sooo much more.

Brax somehow knew what made me ache, what made me hot. He could make me come as easily as he could kiss me. When I was with him, I lost track of the number of orgasms he gave me, the places he touched me. And still it wasn't enough. The clamps showed his dominance, but secretly I craved even more. Needed something I couldn't name.

My body wasn't broken. The pleasure I felt with him was proof of that. There was a deep well of sexual need that even he had yet to reach. What the hell was wrong with me? What could still be missing?

Brax touched me and I trembled. My body was whole again. But my mind? My heart? My soul? I wasn't so sure about the rest of me. And maybe that's why this would be all there could ever be between us. Sex. Raw. Hot. No-strings-attached sex.

Agony blossomed inside my mind like a sudden explosion of fireworks, but I forced it down, back into its cage. This wasn't the time or the place. I didn't want to feel those things now. I didn't want to think about the past, or the future.

I just wanted to feel and he was doing an excellent job of that. I panted, trying to settle into the heat, the burn, the bite of pain. The sweetest pleasure.

I didn't realize my eyes were closed until Brax's palm came to rest against my cheek, his thumb gently brushing away a single tear that had escaped in defiance of my orders.

"Are you sure you want to be here, Miranda? While I can see your pussy is dripping in need for me, you are... quiet. We can stop now." Brax's voice was gentle, and I knew he meant what he said. This was an agreement for our mutual pleasure, nothing more. I wasn't about to tell him all my fears. He already knew too much about my past.

More than anyone else on this planet. More, even, than Natalie.

"No, Master. I don't wish to stop. I need this. I need you."

Brax leaned down and kissed me, gently. There was acceptance in the touch, and I knew he would accept my words and not push for answers. Just as I didn't demand answers from him about where he disappeared to on his missions, when he would return, or if he was fucking someone else. He wasn't my mate, after all.

The kiss turned hot and I trembled. Leaning forward, I felt the gems sway. I lifted my arms to his chest, stealing the touch I knew he would deny me later.

His hands wrapped around my wrists and he lifted my hands above my head, denying me now.

"Come, Miranda." Brax didn't use the term I'd heard other males use with their mates, *gara*. There was no literal translation into English, so my NPU didn't substitute anything when they said it. Best I could figure it was something close to *love*. When I'd asked Roark about the term, he'd said it meant literally a piece of his soul. So romantic, and one more reminder of what Brax and I were to each other. We took care of each other's physical needs, but we weren't the same soul.

Not even close. And that was why I'd never heard that word from his lips.

Obediently, I rose and followed him to a padded bench that was common in the private quarters of males on Trion. Brax had two benches, one narrow, like a sawhorse, that he could bend me over and then chain my wrists to my ankles, leaving my pussy and ass exposed. The other, a padded swing with places for my back, arms and legs so he could strap me in, suspended in the air, and do with me as he pleased.

I loved them both.

Tonight, he led me to the swing, and I fought for patience as he strapped my arms and legs to leather bindings that hung from chains attached to the ceiling. Once I was bound, he nudged my ankles wide, making my pussy open, then lowered me slowly backward until my feet left the ground and I was swinging, face up, in the air. Standing between my open legs, he loomed over me like a sex god and my pussy clenched.

"Don't you want to know what else your gifts can do?" he asked, his gaze roaming over me. I knew he could see my clamped nipples, the turgid tips a deep red. My pussy was bare and open to him, crowned by the green gem that tugged on my clit. I knew he could see how wet I was, how my pussy—and even my ass—clenched in eager anticipation. I wondered if he would fuck me there or place a toy in my ass as he took my pussy. I loved it all. Wanted everything at once.

"Yes, Master. Please." I already knew what the jewels were capable of. I'd heard talk of the special adornments males of this world placed on their females' bodies. Things that vibrated and zapped and wreaked havoc on her sanity. He could wreak some serious havoc on me. I was more than ready. It seemed the clamps were only the start.

If only they were permanent.

Mine.

With a grin I'd become all too familiar with, he touched the large ring he wore on his right hand. With a small twist, tiny electric shots blasted through my clit and nipples, followed by a vibration that made my back arch up and my breath catch.

"Holy shit, what is that?" I gasped. He grinned. I tried to shift my hips, but the swing held me in such a way that I could do nothing but take what he gave me. "I'm going to come, Master."

"No, you will not." His stern order was followed by a swat to my inner thigh, just hard enough to pull me back from the edge. "You will not come until I give you permission."

Moaning, I obeyed, fighting the surge of unexpected heat flowing through my veins.

For him, I would hold on, knowing that in the end, my restraint would be worth it.

Brax bent over me, his dark eyes lingering on the jewels dangling from my nipples. He ran his finger along the inner folds of my pussy and gently tugged on the jewel there.

I couldn't stop the moan that escaped.

"You will look beautiful one day, Miranda, when your mate adorns you properly." His fingertips traced a line from one breast to the other. "A chain will be here." He ran his finger down to my clit as I fought the swing to get closer to him. "And here, shining like a beacon against your skin. No one will doubt you are truly claimed."

He spread my pussy lips apart and placed his huge cock at the edge of my core. The swing was the exact height to allow him to slide right into me. "I'm going to fuck you now. You will not come until I am deep inside you."

He thrust forward, slowly, drawing out my pleasure. One more tap to the ring—which was the smallest remote control I'd ever seen—and another strike of lightning went through my body.

His cock bottomed out inside me, stretching me fully, filling me completely. Making me whole. Then, as I'd come to expect, he reached beneath me and slid two large fingers inside my ass, stretching me as he thrust with his cock. I was full, the sting of pain, the invasion of every part of me making me cry out. I lost it, the orgasm rushing through me like every cell in my body went into spasm.

This bliss, this pleasure he could give me, was like a drug. I was addicted, and I wasn't sure how I could resist another hit. But I would. I would have to because I didn't belong to him.

And as much as I had hoped otherwise, the words he'd just spoken made my body burn but my heart break. I didn't belong to him. And he didn't belong to me.

2

*D*octer Valck Brax

MIRANDA WAS SO BEAUTIFUL, lost to the world as I fucked her through the first spasms of orgasm. She was so hot, so tight and the way her pussy rippled around me as she came would be my undoing. My release would be quick this first time, my balls too full, but it wouldn't be the last. I would take her often this night, and this would be the first of many orgasms. It had to be enough to hold us both over for a few weeks, until I returned from duty once again.

But the sight of her now would keep me warm on long, cold nights, give me a vision to recall when I gripped my cock and found relief while I was gone. The layered dressing gown she wore looked like a gift-wrapped bow made of prisms. And inside that gift, a warm, wet female all too eager to ride my cock. With the gems and clamps peeking out from between the folds... *fark*, I wanted to come again.

Those jewels, the dark green color, lay perfectly against

her skin. I'd chosen them carefully, chastising myself for a fool even as I imagined adorning her in truth. Claiming her for my own. Seeing them on her responsive body, watching my cock slide in and out of her wet pussy as she gasped and begged for more, made me realize that I was lost. I was hers. There would be no fighting it, not any longer.

The problem was that she didn't want me. She didn't want a mate at all. She'd been poorly treated and no longer trusted a mate to care for her. I had been careful, very, very careful not to push her too hard outside of the bedroom. Within, she was mine. She bent to my will and offered her submissive body for my pleasure. But beyond my bedchamber? She was defiant. Quiet. Closed off. Even here, she cried and would not reveal her pain to me.

If I pushed, she would run, just as she'd run from her first mate.

She'd left him behind, on Earth, so desperate to get away that she'd traveled across the galaxy to a new planet.

To me.

And I didn't want to lose her as that fool had.

Miranda had come to me months ago, told me of her trouble finding physical pleasure, of her former mate's lack of skill in the art of satisfying his female. The imbecile. She had blamed herself for his deficiency, but I knew the truth of it. Her mate had been lazy. Selfish. He had not treasured, nor valued her enough to learn what made her happy. To make her writhe and scream and shudder at his every touch.

I had more than made up for his idiocy and enjoyed every moment. Now, with my cock buried deep and her soft skin on display, I mourned both the fact that Miranda did not want me, and the fact that I could not take a mate. My job was too dangerous, and I refused to place a female in the position of being alone for weeks at a time.

But I could not walk away from my duty. The things I did in service to Councilor Roark were important to keep our people safe and protected.

I was torn in half every time I was with Miranda. Wanting to stay with her, adorn her permanently, make her mine. And yet, I wanted to keep her apart. Separate. Safely away from my job and the constant danger I faced. She'd come to me first, offering her body. In all this time, she had not asked me to belong to her. To make her mine permanently. She had not made any demands, either. She simply reveled in the pleasure I provided, as did I.

I could not dwell on this now, my cock buried deep, her inner walls gripping and practically milking the cum from my balls. A good lover did not think of anything but the sweet bliss of a female's body at a time like this. I was an attentive lover, and I would prove that to her.

I let the swing do the work. Putting my hands on the chains that affixed it to the ceiling, I pushed. She slipped off my cock until only the tip remained opening her up, then I let go, allowing gravity to slide her back onto me. Again and again did she swing off, then onto my cock until her breathing was erratic. Sweat glistened on her skin. Her pussy juices coated my balls. A flush crept over her adorned breasts. She was being such a good girl holding off her second orgasm. Waiting. *Waiting.*

"Come now," I growled, unable to hold off my own pleasure any longer. It sizzled down my spine, burst from me in spurts of thick cum that filled her. She screamed and came with me, taking everything I gave her with unleashed passion, with the most giving heart, the most willing body.

I held my legs locked, trying to stop myself from crumpling to the floor. She could kill me with pleasure alone, but I had to care for her, see to her needs before my own, remove her from the swing and carry her back to bed. I would gently remove the clamps and kiss the places that had been so beautifully tortured. Then I would lick her clit until she came again.

Long minutes later, job complete, I settled her against me, her taste on my tongue, her juices coating my cock. *Fark.*

Miranda was wrapped in my arms, replete. Exhausted. Covered in the sweaty, sated haze of sex.

I loved the way she curled against me. Trusted me to hold her. A small smile turned up the corner of her full lips, and it made me smile, too. I was... happy. Content. The feeling was usually as fleeting as an orgasm, but the contentment I felt with her had extended to include this... *snuggle time,* as she'd called it.

I could not keep her with me any more than I could hold on to the feelings she pulled from my body. And so circumstances forced me to break the mood. Usually, I was in the city for several days after a mission, free time I would spend with my cock buried deep in Miranda, making her come until she couldn't speak.

Not this time. I was back in the city tonight only, for duty called. "I must leave in the morning."

She tensed, her body going rigid in surprise as if she were suddenly uncomfortable, but she did not lift her head from my chest. "So soon?"

"Councilor Roark is sending me to deal with a problem in the south."

She relaxed in my arms once again, and I pulled the soft sheet up to cover us both, not wanting her tender skin to get cold. "Do you think you will ever be done with these missions, Brax? Ever settle down and take a mate?"

It was my turn to go still. What was she asking? Was she asking me to be hers? She'd asked if I would ever *take a mate,* not take *her* as a mate. My heart skipped a beat, then raced with excitement I had not expected to feel. A longing for something I'd never wanted before. "Are you... are you asking me to be yours, Miranda? Your mate? To retire from field duty?"

She turned her head, glanced up at me. "What? No. I would never ask you to do that. I wouldn't want to put any pressure on you."

That quickly, my excitement faded to disappointment. Perhaps I had not pleasured her well enough. Perhaps she simply didn't want me to be hers forever. She'd come to me with one goal, to know if her body was broken, to know if she could experience pleasure. Perhaps all she'd ever wanted from me was an answer to that question. Oh, I'd answered it all right. If she had any doubts of her passionate nature, how beautiful and incredible she was when she was in the throes of it, how hot I became knowing I was the one to make her that way... I'd spank her ass until she couldn't sit for a week.

"I will continue to serve as long as Roark needs me." I kept my voice even, pushing all emotion down. Away.

"Of course." She snuggled in and turned her head, placing a kiss on my chest. A kiss that caused my heart to ache with a pain I'd never felt before. "I would never ask you to give up anything for me. That wasn't the deal we made."

No, it was not, but I had believed—no, hoped. I had hoped that when my fighting days were done I would make her mine. Claim her. Fill her with children and adorn her with gold and jewels, as a proper mate should. I'd lied when I told her the jewels that had decorated her lush body so beautifully were a gift for her.

They were a gift for *me*. I had needed to see her wearing something that marked her as mine, even if it was a lie. Even if they weren't permanent. *Yet*.

Earth females were a mystery. I'd only met Natalie, Roark's mate, and that had not helped me with my understanding of their minds when it came to choosing mates.

But Roark and Natalie had been matched through the Interstellar Brides Program. Perhaps that was why they seemed to move in and out of each other's space seamlessly, as if they were one person. One soul.

I would never ask you to give up anything for me.

Never.

That was a gods damned long time.

Ignoring the ache spreading in my chest, I stroked her shoulder and placed a kiss on top of her head. "I must head south in the morning. I will be gone several weeks. I wanted you to know."

"Okay."

I knew that meant she understood and was not upset I would be leaving. That Earth slang I had picked up from her and Natalie over the two years since their initial arrival providing me the comprehension I required. But that one word of simple agreement also hurt.

My lips lingered in her hair, the dark softness a soothing balm against my skin. I could stay here, holding her, forever. But that was not to be my fate. I had to leave in the morning, a rise in illegal weapons trade on the southern coast required my attention. Roark had asked me to take care of it himself.

People were dying in the smaller cities, victims of territorial wars between smugglers' factions. It had to be stopped.

A soldier would be easily identified and killed if he tried to enter the smugglers' camp.

But a doctor? I'd be recruited. Taken to the inner circle. Trusted to treat their mates and children, heal their wounds.

They wouldn't see me as a threat until it was too late.

It seemed no one expected much of me. Not the smugglers. And not the female who had fallen asleep in my arms. My chest was wet beneath her eyes, a sign of more tears.

Even in that, I was not trusted. Miranda was hurting, yet she didn't trust me with her truths. Her hurts. Only with her body. All I was to her was... *okay*.

When I returned from my next mission, I would do everything in my power to convince her that okay wasn't enough. I wanted her to be mine. I wanted to hear a *yes* from her lips, not only when I brought her to orgasm, but when I asked her to be my mate, my partner in bed and out. And if that meant I had to tie her down and give her a thousand orgasms, break barriers down until she was a sobbing, sweaty, exhausted mess and that one word would be uttered again and again, I would.

She was mine. She simply did not know it yet.

3

Miranda, Personal Quarters, Xalia City, Five Weeks Later

"Okay, girlfriend, I brought the wine."

Natalie held up a bottle of pale liquid and walked past me into my quarters. I'd sent her a comms message and she had appeared—thankfully not empty-handed—in less than an hour. With a newborn, a toddler and a *very* attentive mate, I was impressed she'd torn herself away so quickly.

The door to my quarters silently slid closed behind her, and I followed her into my small kitchen area. Thank god for BFFs, even on Trion. I couldn't even imagine if I'd remained on Earth without her. Here, even on a planet we were growing accustomed to, we'd needed each other. Of course, she had hottie Roark. And little Noah, who wasn't so dang little anymore, not with Roark's genes in him. And then baby Talia. I grinned, thinking about how much trouble Roark was going to be in soon enough. She was only five weeks old and that little girl had her daddy wrapped around her little finger, just like her mama.

"The bottle's a little different than on Earth, but the wine tastes the same," Natalie continued, reaching for glasses and setting them on the counter. She was a mother of two, and she still looked amazing. She was everything I was not... tall. Blonde. Gorgeous.

I had mousy brown hair and unremarkable features. I wasn't particularly beautiful, my nose was too long, my chin was too pointy, my left eye was slightly bigger than my right, and I'd never grown out of my gangly teenage phase. Laser surgery had taken care of my near-sightedness when I was just out of high school, but even without the glasses I'd worn most of my life, I still felt like a newborn colt trying to figure out how to walk on wobbly legs. I'd never had that whole *confidence* thing. Since Brax, I was better, but I was still me.

Plain old me.

"I don't think one bottle is going to be enough."

"That bad, huh?" Natalie tilted her head in that sympathetic girlfriend way and made a face. "Well, I know where the chef keeps his stash. I won't tell if you won't."

Natalie held out a fist, her pinky the only finger sticking straight out. "Pinky swear?"

I laughed, I couldn't help it. "Pinky swear."

We hooked our small fingers and shook on our new oath. Thank goodness she knew when I sent out the SOS that alcohol would be required. This was exactly what I needed. A big bottle of wine and a chance to cry, scream and get drunk. We'd been friends back on Earth. I'd followed her to Trion when she mated Roark. Natalie had insisted I accompany her and Noah. Since Roark was a councilor, he'd been able to approve the transfer on the spot. I'd been on the planet with Natalie for two years and could now make Cookies and Cream ice cream from the S-gen machine. I drove Natalie's staff crazy, but I loved to bake and had mastered the art of *poofing* flour, eggs, butter and the fixings for chocolate chip cookies or snickerdoodles—there was a reason I was Noah's favorite Auntie—but I didn't have the same inside track for the good alcohol. The *real* booze. The liquid gold she was pouring liberally into the glasses, thank god.

I needed a vat of it. An IV right to my heart.

Even though it was my quarters we were in, she turned and handed me a very full glass as if she were the hostess. While there weren't grapes on Trion, there was another kind of oddly named fruit that was fermented. I wasn't a connoisseur by any means, picking up the smoky notes and all that, but my taste buds knew a good wine when it hit them and this stuff packed a punch.

Natalie took her own glass, full to nearly the top, and plopped down on my sofa. "Okay. Spill."

As I dropped down onto the sofa in my living area beside her, we both knew she wasn't talking about the wine.

Sighing, I bent my knees and tucked my legs up beneath me. It had been over a month since I'd last seen Brax and I missed him. Terribly. "It's Brax."

"Of course it is." Natalie looked at me with nothing but sympathy in her blue eyes. "Did you talk to him today? What did he say to you? That jerk, I'll strangle him if he wasn't good to you."

"What? When? I thought he was out on a mission." What the hell was she talking about? Brax was here? In the city?

And he hadn't called me?

Oblivious to my pain, Natalie kept talking. "He was here,

last night, giving his report. I assumed he told you he was leaving again tomorrow, and that's why you were upset." Her raised brows and matter-of-fact voice made me feel like I'd just swallowed an entire bucket of ice. Brax had been... *was* here, in the city? He was alive and well and hadn't seen me in weeks.

I shook my head and took a gulp of wine. "No, that's not why."

Maybe it would have been, if he'd contacted me.

But he hadn't called. Not once. No messages. No comms. Nothing. I'd been in total communications blackout for the last five weeks trying to focus on my little students, worried sick, imagining him dead and rotting in the sand, lost in the middle of the desert. I'd imagined scorpions climbing in and out of his eye sockets—and they didn't even have scorpions on Trion. I'd been going crazy with worry, thinking I'd made a mistake the last time I saw him, thinking I'd misread his words. Waiting for him to get home so I could ask him once and for all to be mine. And he'd been *here? Home? In the city and NOT calling me?*

"Shit." I didn't normally cuss, at least not out loud, but this was too much for my brain to process and keep control of my mouth at the same time.

The last time I was with Brax, I'd fallen asleep in his arms, too blissed out on sex swing induced orgasms to do anything else. When I woke up, he, too, was asleep. He'd said our time was short, that he'd leave again in the morning.

The idea of watching him walk away—again—had been too much. I hadn't been able to be there when he left. *Again.*

And after what he'd said, when he'd been fucking me as I'd been tied to that swing—*you will look beautiful one day, Miranda, when your mate adorns you properly*—I knew I couldn't stay. Couldn't say goodbye. I had come to realize that he had no intention of ever being my mate. He spoke openly of another male taking on that role even while he'd been buried balls deep inside me.

He intended me for another. Not for him.

And so I'd left, sneaked out in the middle of the night. For the first time in all the months we'd had sex, I'd done the walk of shame. Felt that our *friends with benefits* arrangement was... cheap.

I took a big gulp of wine. Then another.

"Okaaaay." Natalie dragged out the word. "Then what's up?"

"I think you were right," I said finally.

Her mouth dropped open and she stared, wide-eyed. "What time is it?"

"What?" I asked, frowning. "Eight-thirty? Why?"

"Because you *never* say I'm right. I want to get this on record."

I rolled my eyes and laughed, took a gulp of the wine. "Whatever. I'm done."

"Done? With what?"

"Friends with benefits."

Understanding crossed her face. "Why? The sex isn't good anymore?"

I thought of Brax and the way he moved his hips. How he could work his tongue in some magical way that made my eyes cross. The way he filled me up, took his time, had claimed me completely, in every way. Front, back and sideways. He knew every single inch of my body, intimately. My pussy clenched just thinking about him. My nipples had been sore for days from the jeweled nipple clamps he'd used. *Adorned me with.* He said he liked to see me adorned, that they were gifts to me. And yet I'd left them on his bedside table. For the next female he took to his bed.

Based on the way his cock hardened as I squirmed when he'd put them on, he liked seeing me with them on, seeing the effect they had on me. He knew it made me hot, made me wet, made me beg for it rough. Wild and untamed.

"Hello? Earth to Mira?" The laughter in Natalie's eyes made it clear she knew *exactly* what I'd been thinking about.

"Yeah, sex is not the problem," I replied, squirming on the couch. The sexy little outfit I'd worn that night was buried in a drawer. Tonight, I had on some Trion-style loose pants and a good, old-fashioned Earth t-shirt. My hair I'd put up in a messy bun. "God, if it got any better, I might not survive."

Natalie grinned. We didn't talk all that much about her sex life; Roark was ridiculously possessive, but I knew she was never left unsatisfied. Having had a baby recently, I imagined she should still be sitting on an ice pack and trying to remember the last time she'd showered. One thing Trion had over Earth were those sweet ReGen pods. Two hours after having Talia, she had been completely recovered. I had no doubt she and Roark had already been practicing for baby number three.

And yet I didn't even have a male who wanted me for more than sex. Oh, I'd *asked* for the arrangement with Brax, so I didn't feel used. Hell, I'd used Brax's cock as much as he'd used me. But I wasn't his mate, had only been adorned temporarily. I knew Natalie was adorned with all the customary jewelry of a Trion mate. Nipple rings—not just the jeweled nipple clamps Brax used on me—and a thin chain running between them with Roark's medallion. It was hidden beneath her clothing, but sometimes the outlines of the *adornments* were visible. And more than once, on special occasions, she wore gowns designed to *show them off*. Sexy, flowing pieces of clothing that made her look like a sex goddess.

When it came to exuding sex like a Trion female, Natalie had it *down*.

If we weren't on a strange planet having sex with aliens, I'd think we were living in some kind of desert sheik porno. All we needed to do was go to Outpost Two, in the middle of the desert, to make the scenario complete. That's where the leaders on the continent gathered for their meetings. Roark had dragged us along once. Well, insisted Natalie and Noah accompany him. I'd been the tag-a-long. And to be perfectly honest, I loved the tents and the piercings—or *adornments*— as the women here called them. They were intimate and taboo and hit all my hot buttons. But the sand? Umm... no. The sand I could do without.

Whatever. It turned out I *liked* sheik porno, especially with my own super-sexy, super-dominant sheik. Or doctor.

"Sex isn't enough anymore," I said, finishing off my glass and reaching for the bottle to give it a refill.

She tilted her head, eyed me. Her glass was still full. I wasn't sure if she could drink and nurse, but maybe she was just holding the cup for me, because when I was done with the bottle, I'd be emptying her glass, too. Didn't want to waste any.

"You fell for him." She wasn't asking.

"Wouldn't you?" I countered, taking another sip of wine. I could feel the effects of it kicking in, the loose limbs, the warmth seeping into my veins.

She cocked her head to the side. "I understand. I have Roark. And no, sex wouldn't be enough. I wanted it all."

"You got it, too." My words weren't snarky or laced with jealousy, but I wanted what she had. A mate of her own to come home to after working. To cuddle with. To have his babies. A mate who would protect me and make me feel safe. A mate who would adorn me with his permanent nipple rings. And chains. And maybe even a piercing in my clit. I squirmed some more.

Did I know the thoughts chasing each other around in my skull were crazy? Yes. But I wanted to feel the tug on my nipples when my mate was somewhere else. I wanted to feel the gentle pull and know the man who adorned me would return. The adornments on Trion were a symbol of love. Of respect. Of claiming. They enhanced a woman's beauty, made her feel special. And beautiful. And on top of all that, the adornments were a connection. A formal binding.

Permanent. Real.

And that's what I told Natalie. "When he put the nipple clamps on me, I was reminded of what I'm missing. The temporariness of our arrangement." I leaned back with a sigh, and I knew my voice held every ounce of regret I was feeling. How the hell had I let myself fall for a man who didn't really want me... *again.* "He's amazing, but he's out of town as fast as the nipple clamps come off after sex."

"He's a busy doctor," she replied, as if his job would justify his lack of commitment.

"He's more than a doctor and you know it." I stared at her, hoping maybe she'd know some top-secret stuff about what Brax did since she was mated to the councilor. But she remained silent.

I sighed. "Roark is a councilor. His schedule is insane, but he finds time for you. For Noah and now Talia. He *makes* time." When she was about to say more, I kept going. "Roark puts energy and focus into the things he wants. Things which are important to him. Things that are a priority."

"Brax puts energy and focus into sex with you," she

replied, her voice soothing. "Hell, woman, I've seen you after. You're like a puddle of goo."

My cheeks heated, and I wasn't sure if it was from the wine or her words. But the last time I'd been with Brax, even after I'd been swing fucked, I hadn't been a puddle of goo. My emotions that night had completely ruined the sex buzz. Dammit.

"I need more than sex," I countered. "If he wanted me *completely,* then he'd put his all into being with me. I want it all, Nat. I want what you have with Roark. I'm ready now. I wasn't when we first came to Trion, but I'm ready now."

"He's a good one, Miranda. Have you told him how you feel?"

"I asked him when he was going to be ready to take a mate."

That got her attention. "And? What did he say?"

"That he would serve Roark for as long as he was needed."

She slumped back, her outward disappointment a mirror for my internal state. "That's romantic."

"Yeah, and it was about a minute after he told me he could only be with me for one night because he was leaving again. For even longer this time."

"I shouldn't say anything, but Roark's having a problem with some pirates on the southern coast. It's a big problem. Women and children are dying." That explanation should have come from Brax, not Natalie. I'd watched and admired military families back on Earth who waited for a loved one to serve. I would have waited for Brax. I would have understood and supported his decision to protect and serve his people. But he didn't give me that choice. He gave me no choices except keep things as they were... or end it.

"He should have told me. Maybe I'm crazy. I know it's

weird, but I want my life to be like an eighties movie. I want the grand gesture. I want him to throw everything on the line for me. No holding back. Total devotion. I deserve that."

"You do. We all do."

I sighed and took another gulp of wine, decided one bottle was definitely not going to be enough. "I think I need some kind of weird soundtrack or something. I want him to hold the boom box up for me."

Natalie was taking another *sip* of wine. Apparently, my last bit of ranting about Brax had broken her resolve to defend him. "They don't have boom boxes here."

"I didn't mean it literally." I took a swing of wine, nodded my head. "But sex isn't enough. I'm worth more, and I'm going to get it. Staying with Brax for the fun and hot sex is only keeping me away from *him*."

She leaned forward, eyes wide. "Him? Him who? Have you met someone else?"

I sighed, looked down at my glass and realized it was empty. Again. I grabbed the bottle and poured more. Poured it *all*. "There is no specific him," I clarified. "A mate. A real future. A family of my own. It's time for me to get bride tested."

At my words, she nearly bounced off the couch. "Tested? God, that was so hot. Oooh, who do you think you'd get? An Everian? I heard they're ridiculously fast."

"Aren't they marked or something?" I looked down at my palm. No odd birthmark.

"I know!" she shouted, making me jump. "Viken. *Three* hotties."

"Three? Um, I don't think I could handle that." I thought of sex with Brax and that was pretty intense. Two might be... wow. My brain stalled. One in front of me, taking my pussy. Another behind, holding me down, filling my ass as they played. My body lit up. Two could be really hot. But three? No. I wasn't so sure about three.

"Fine, then you could have a beast. I bet their cocks are huge."

I laughed then, practically snorting wine out my nose. "You are mated to a huge Trion alien. I can only assume by the size of him that his cock is more than enough for you."

Her eyes went all dreamy. "Oh, yes."

"Stop squirming," I scolded, knowing she was getting all hot just thinking about Roark's cock. I loved him like a brother... but yuck. Just, no.

However, the contented, happy smile on Natalie's face made me want a mate of my own all the more. Brax's cock was serious business, but it wasn't mine. He'd made that very clear. If I couldn't have that thick, long piece of alien cock to myself forever and ever, then I was going to get one that I *could* keep.

"Sign me up. I want to get matched." I stood, went over to the door. "I want my own cock, one I can keep."

"Now?" she asked. Realizing I was serious, she stood as well. "You're insane, you know that? It's not just a cock. It's an alien. A mate who will be possessive and growly."

"Now you're just teasing me." Growly and *possessive.* That was what I wanted. I was tired of being a booty-call. An unwanted wife. A back-up, maybe later, friend men slept with. I wanted a man who *wanted* to be with me. Who wanted it more than he wanted to breathe. I wanted a man who loved me the way Roark loved Natalie. Complete and utter devotion. Adoration. Growly and possessive sound fucking perfect.

"You'll have to leave me. You know that? What if you get sent to Prillon Prime? Or the Colony? Somewhere far, far away." Natalie walked closer and gave me a bear hug, squeezing the last two years of love and friendship into me between one breath and the next. "Never mind that. I'm totally being selfish. I want you to be happy, but I'm going to miss you."

"Me, too." I shrugged. "Maybe I'll get matched to Trion." I waggled my eyebrows and looked Natalie dead in the eyes until she laughed out loud. I could deal with that. I loved this place. The dominant males. The adornments. The sexy clothing and sex goddess attitude of the females here. But the truth of it was, I loved Earth, too. It wasn't about the place for me, it was about the people. I could be happy on the moon if I had a devoted mate with me.

"Okay. But are you sure about this? Once you sign up, you can't take it back. It's a totally legal, binding contract. You'll be married... mated, whatever, as soon as you take the test."

I squeezed her one more time and stepped back. "I know, but it's been over a month and you said Brax was back in town. He didn't even bother to call. It's time to move on. I want a real mate. I'm ready for a grown-up relationship. I'm tired of casual sex. And I'm tired of sitting by the phone, waiting for a call that never comes."

"They don't have phones here."

"Whatever. You know what I mean. I'm tired of being *that* girl."

"But you're drunk."

"Girlfriend, it takes more than two glasses of wine. I can drink you under the table, remember?" It was my turn to laugh.

"Right. I forgot." Natalie was smiling, too.

"Besides, I'm not driving a car, I'm getting bride tested. And right now feels like the perfect time to do something insane."

Natalie took my wine glass and set it next to hers on the counter. "Okay, girlfriend. First, we're going to get you some coffee."

We hit up the S-Gen machine and I waited for the caffeine jolt to kick in. When I was a hundred and ten percent sure I was sober, I met her gaze and nodded. I was done with waiting around, second guessing and hoping for what I couldn't have. It was time to get matched to my perfect mate. If he was on Trion, great. If not? So be it. I'd miss Natalie and the kids, but that's what comms were for. "Ready."

"Okay. Let's do this." She placed her arm around my shoulder and walked me to the processing center to be matched to my perfect mate. She leaned in close as we approached the door to the medical center where the testing would take place. "And I won't say a word about the wine."

aptain Trist Treval, Sector 17, Battleship Zakar

I LEANED over the battle map, the ever-present tension in my shoulders and neck a constant reminder that the war with the Hive was not won, that my warriors were out there dying. Still. Always.

"We've destroyed their scout ships, Captain, but the larger attack vessels just disappeared." Captain Wyle spoke on my right. He was an experienced fighter who brought true honor to Prillon Prime. If he said the Hive ship vanished before his eyes, I believed him.

"Did you see one of the new destroyers?" I asked.

The new advanced ships developed by the Hive had recently begun arriving in other sectors. They were invisible to sensors and impossible to track. I'd never seen one, but he had. He knew what to look for, to know if that new threat was here, in this battlegroup. The Coalition Fleet had lost

Battlegroup Varsten in Sector 438 before Battlegroup Karter and a fighting unit from the Intelligence Core had managed to eliminate the threat in Sector 437 under Commander Karter. Our assigned sector was nowhere near them, but with the Hive, nothing was ever that easy. And their new technology was being deployed throughout the galaxy much faster than we'd anticipated.

I hated the Hive.

"No," he replied. "They were too small, but there were at least three of them. Enough to cause a serious problem." Captain Wyle pointed to a planet on the star map. He'd been out there, flying with his warriors, when the battle happened. He was our best pilot, and leader of our airborne fighters. "We had a line-of-sight visual, but they ran behind the fourth planet and we lost them."

Across from us, Commander Grigg Zakar cursed and slammed his fist down on the flat screen we stood before. "Gods be damned. Prime Nial warned us about their new cloaking technology. But I had hoped that with the destruction of the Hive ship in Sector 437, we wouldn't have to deal with this yet."

"The Hive are one mind, Commander." The reminder was not needed, but I had not shared the same hope. I was a realist. Commander Zakar had been in charge of this battlegroup for more than twenty years. I'd been his second in command for long enough to know that despite everything he'd seen, he still had hope. We all did. He fought like a warrior who believed he could win. But then, he had a mate. He needed hope, needed to believe in a future for her and their children.

All I had, all I knew, was war. Killing. Watching thousands of new recruits come out of the Coalition Academy and from the member planets' recruitment facilities to fight and die. Or worse, be taken alive by the Hive and converted into the enemy. *Contaminated.*

"Get the I.C. on comms. I want to know exactly how we fight this thing." Grigg was dark, even for a Prillon, his lineage that of an ancient family that had defended this sector of space for hundreds of years. His skin and hair were brown, his eyes a blend of red and orange his Earth mate called "rust".

While both Prillon, we were nothing alike, he and I, neither in temperament nor in looks. My family line was fair. Golden from head to toe. But where he was revered on the home world as something akin to royalty, I was no one, a third son whose two fathers had both paid the ultimate price in this war. They'd died fighting while I was in the academy, and I'd vowed to destroy as many Hive warriors as I could. I'd vowed to fight, as had my two older brothers. We'd stood side by side in our family home and sworn to protect our two younger sisters and our mother, who were now safely back on the home world. Prillon Prime remained safe because of us. Because of everyone who fought.

My brothers and I had scattered days later, gone to serve, sent to different sectors of space. Like me, they fought on. Still. But I'd made my own oath that day, to my dead fathers, to the gods, to myself. I'd vowed to kill Hive with every breath, including my last. And I had no intention of breaking that promise.

Behind me, the comms officer answered. "I'll get I.C. for you, but it'll take me some time, Commander."

"Fuck that. Get me Commander Karter, instead. Sector 437." Grigg was pacing now, his arms crossed as he stared down at the star map broken into a grid. This was our home.

Our area to defend. And the Zakar family had not lost ground to the Hive in hundreds of years. We had no intention of starting now. "Gods damned I.C. won't tell me what I need to know anyway."

That made me grin. Grigg wasn't wrong. Spies and their secrets. I didn't like their games. I preferred to acquire a target and take it out. In that, Grigg and I were very much alike.

We waited a few moments, but the comms officer made a startled sound. "I'm sorry. Captain Trist, there is an incoming message for you."

I turned around and walked to the control station, leaned over the officer's shoulder. "From who?"

He looked a little uncomfortable. Odd. "Um, Trion, sir."

What? I didn't know anyone on Trion. It was an odd planet with an odd people. They lived in tents, from what I understood. Primitives who liked to place metal piercings in their females and treat them more like pets than mates of worth. I did not understand their philosophies, but I could not argue that their females were well-protected and taken care of. And Trion males were fierce and worthy fighters. Still, I knew no one from that world. "Well?"

The comms officer stiffened as Captain Wyle and Commander Zakar came from behind to stand on either side of me. "Captain Trist Treval of Prillon Prime, this is the Interstellar Brides Processing Center in Xalia City, planet Trion. I have your matched mate awaiting transport. This communication is intended to confirm your coordinates per Interstellar Brides Program protocol."

"What?"

"Am I speaking to Captain Trist, or his commanding officer?" The matter-of-fact voice sounded bored, as if this happened dozens of times a day. But not to me. It had never happened to me.

Grigg was grinning. "This is Commander Zakar. I can confirm Captain Trist's location. Initiate transport."

"Thank you, Commander. Transport will begin momentarily. Trion out."

The comm went dead and I stood, stunned. Seconds ticked by, then the commander slapped me on the back. Hard. "Congratulations, Trist."

Mate? I had a mate? I'd been matched? To a Trion female?

Captain Wyle was smiling like he'd just made a kill. "Fuck me, Trist. An Interstellar Bride." He slapped me on the other side of my back. Harder. "Lucky fuck."

TRIST, Transport Room 3, Battleship Zakar

I STOOD ALONE before the transport pad, the transport tech the only other person in the room. The commander had been more than happy to dismiss me to see to my mate. Captain Wyle seemed almost... jealous as I left. I didn't know what to think, didn't understand. Why me? Why now? It had been five years since I'd been tested. Five long years of waiting, and I'd pretty much given up all hope. I'd stopped wondering ages ago if I would ever have a bride. I had assumed I was an impossible bastard and a true match would never be found.

But now? Fuck. Somehow, I had remembered to go to my quarters and retrieve two collars from my drawer, the place I'd shoved them when Nevo had requested to be released from our agreement. When Captain Myntar's second had been lost to the Hive, the captain, along with his mate and son, had been left behind to go on alone. His second's death was the very reason every Prillon male chose a second. No female or her children were ever left alone and unprotected.

The tragedy meant Captain Drake Myntar's family had needed a second protector. Drake was third on command in the battlegroup, a good friend, and I could no more deny a female and child protection than I could deny my friend a chance at happiness. Lady Mara Myntar was a beautiful Prillon female and she'd accepted Nevo with open arms. The new family had been together for more than two years, their bond strong.

I was happy for Nevo but had not bothered to find another Prillon second. As I hadn't thought I'd ever be matched, I hadn't considered anyone for the role.

Now I was out of time. The hum of the incoming transport vibrated through my body and my mate was appearing. Now.

In the blink of an eye, she was there. Sprawled across the metal raised floor was a naked female. Her face was delicate and beautiful. Exceptionally feminine in comparison to the sharp angles of mine. Her hair was long and darker than wine, a deep brown that I found fascinating. I couldn't wait to see that dark silk spread out across my golden chest. Her curves tempted me to reach out and stroke her skin here. Now. Her breasts were large and full, the nipples a deep pink that matched her lips.

I longed to spread her thighs wide and find out if her pussy was pink as well. Or brown. Or golden.

Something primal in me woke, something I'd never felt before. *Possessive.* My cock went instantly hard and my entire body grew tense with the need to protect. Mate. Claim.

Mine.

"Turn your back!" I growled and leapt up onto the platform to shield her from the view of the transport tech. Out of the corner of my eye, I saw him spin about and stare at the far wall.

I knew from other mates who'd been sent from the Brides Program that the females were transported without clothing, leaving behind all vestiges of their previous planet. It was a Prillon tradition, a way to ensure the female was fully prepared to be immersed in Prillon life.

But now, with my mate before me, unconscious, vulnerable and every inch of her soft perfection on display, I did not like it.

"Get me a blanket from the emergency response kit."

I heard the tech move about, but I stared solely at her. I didn't even know her name. I thought to ask the tech who would have received her file from the processing center on Trion, but I decided to wait. I wanted her to tell me. I wanted to know what color her eyes were, and what her voice would sound like when she was crying out my name.

My cock thickened, lengthened with an immediate need for her. She was not adorned as a mated Trion female normally would be, but perhaps it was because she was mated to me. I did not need piercings or chains, jewels or any other fanciful decoration on my mate. Just looking at her lush body was all I needed to be pleased, to be aroused. To be possessive in the extreme.

"Captain?"

"What?" I snarled, curling my body over her so he would not see anything precious.

"Sir, your blanket, but I can't make it up the steps without looking." He was Prillon and understood. I didn't remember if he wore a collar, if he was mated or not. This was a moment I should have shared with a second, but I was thankful for his understanding since I was alone. For now. Finding the beautiful female a second worthy protector would be one of my first priorities—after I'd claimed her. Looking at her now, I knew I could not wait to find a second before making her mine.

I respected the tech's good judgment in attempting to maintain my mate's modesty—and keep his head upon his shoulders—but I didn't want to look away, even for a moment. Irrationally, I worried she might transport away. She was still a dream, a figment of my imagination that I would guard jealously.

It was this wave of jealousy, of fear I might lose her, that caused me to remember the collars. I opened one, the green one of my family, and placed it about my neck. I only felt the heft of it but nothing more.

Per protocol, she must agree to the placement of my collar about her neck. Once she did, I would have thirty days to seduce her. Love her. Give her every reason in the universe to choose to stay with me.

I reached behind me blindly, grateful when I felt the press of one of the soft blankets in my palm. "Thank you."

"Of course, Captain." I heard the heavy boots of the Prillon tech walking back to his station and trusted that he had the good sense to keep his gaze averted. Still, I wrapped her gently in the warmth of the blanket and lifted her into my arms, amazed at the lush softness of her body's curves beneath the material. So soft. By the gods, my cock was painfully hard, aching to fill her.

But first, she must accept my collar. My right to woo her. To protect her. I could not leave this room without the symbol of my protection around her neck. I did not want to fight any challengers for what was mine. With the primitive instincts flaring out of control within me at first sight of her, I might kill anyone who tried to take her from me.

I was a rational male. Battle hardened. Cold. I'd been called detached. Calculated. More machine than male. And yet, when I looked at her, that calm didn't just melt away. It vanished as if someone took a laser cannon to my insides and lit me on fire.

"When will she wake?" I asked. Surely this transport tech had seen other brides arrive and knew how long I would have to wait. Still, my normally inexhaustible patience had abandoned me, along with reason, calm, certainty...

I studied her features, absorbing every detail. Burning her into my mind and memory. All the while, completely absurd thoughts whirled through my mind. What if she opened her eyes and was not pleased with the sight of me? What if I frightened her? What if...

"Usually within a few minutes, Captain."

Thank the gods. I wasn't sure I could maintain control for much longer. She breathed peacefully, but she did not move. What if she were injured? Ill?

"Captain, sir. Sorry to bother, but I need to clear the transport pad. We've got supplies scheduled to arrive from Prillon Prime."

"Of course." I was standing in the middle of the transport area, staring at a small, fragile female. I had lost my senses indeed.

The tech grinned at me as I stepped down and moved toward the exit. "Congratulations, Captain."

"Thank you for your assistance," I told the tech as I walked toward the transport door. I nodded and kept walking. Using one hand, I tucked the blanket up around her neck. If anyone was foolish enough to challenge me between this room and my personal quarters, so be it.

5

HE OFFERED a slight bow before I left the room and moved quickly through the corridors. If anyone thought it odd I carried an unconscious female wrapped solely in a blanket through a battleship, no one said so. Wisely, no one even looked at us curiously as we passed.

They didn't matter. Nothing mattered but my mate. How had I been upset, just a short time ago, to receive word I had been matched? Why had I not wanted this? How had I been so stupid? But I had no second. No one to protect her should anything happen to me.

I growled as I slapped my hand beside the door to my quarters, opening it. I would find a second promptly.

"Oh," she said, her voice soft. Sweet.

"Hello, mate." Happiness and fierce protectiveness swept through me. Mate.

She stirred, tried to wiggle out of my hold.

"Be still. You've transported a long distance."

"I'm heavy."

I laughed at that but entered my private quarters and moved to sit upon the soft chair I used for reading in the evening before bed. Taking my time, I sat, careful not to jostle her. This was a new experience, holding something so precious on my lap. With her tucked into my arms, I was content.

When we were settled, I looked down to find her studying me. There was no fear in her eyes, only curiosity. Acceptance.

"I am Trist. Your mate."

"I'm Miranda." Her gaze dropped to the green collar now affixed around my neck as I rolled her name around in my thoughts.

Miranda.

"Your name is beautiful, Miranda. As are you."

She smiled shyly, her cheeks turning an intriguing shade of pink as she looked around. My quarters were in order. Everything was clean, organized, appropriately stored and prepared for battle. "I was told I was transporting to a battleship."

I nodded, studied the pert tilt of her nose, dark eyebrows. "Yes, you are on Battleship Zakar. I am Captain Trist, second in command. These are my—our—quarters. I will put in for a transfer to a larger room once I have chosen a second."

She didn't react to my comment about choosing a second, and I relaxed, enjoying the moment. Holding her. Feeling her in my arms.

"Where are we? I've never been in space before."

"Sector 17. It is quite a distance from your home world of Trion."

"Oh, um, well, yes. I transported from Trion, but I'm from Earth. Originally, I mean. I've been living on Trion for the last two years."

"You're human?" I asked, full of wonder. That explained the odd colored eyes, her smaller size. She was from Earth, like Lady Zakar. Yet they looked nothing alike.

"Yes."

"Explain your presence on Trion."

She shifted in my hold, and I allowed her to sit up but kept my arms around her. I was content to have her upon my lap, feel her softness, breathe in her scent. My cock, pressed into her hip, and was also quite content as she spoke of her friend, Natalie, who had mated a Trion councilor. She explained that she had escorted Natalie and her new son back to Trion and had made a life there for the past two years.

"So you were on Trion because of a friend, not because you'd been matched to a warrior from that planet?"

She shook her head, then studied me. "No. I wasn't matched to Trion. I was matched to you."

Those words from her lips… gods, they made me want to make her mine even more. I had to get my collar on her. Now. I wanted to know exactly what she was feeling when I saw that look in her eyes.

"It is customary for Prillon warriors and their mates to wear mating collars."

Her gaze dropped to my neck again and she reached up with delicate fingers to trace the material I'd placed around my neck. "I know. I read about it."

"Once I place my collar around your neck, our official mating trial will begin. You will have thirty days to accept my claim or choose another."

"I know."

"Your collar will remain black—unnamed—until you are officially claimed. Once you accept me and my second, your collar will turn green, to match mine, and you will be mine forever."

She bit her lip, the warmth of her touch barely skirting the edge of my collar. That small touch had the muscles in my neck tensing in reaction. Wherever she touched, I burned. "Okay."

"Yes? You accept my right to you for the thirty-day mating period?"

"Yes, Trist. I want the collar. I want to be with you. We were matched. I trust in that. I'm ready."

Shaking at her simple words, I lifted the second collar and placed the slim black band about her neck. When it clicked in place, I felt her.

My chest felt as if it swelled. My uniform was too tight. I couldn't breathe. And yet, I held on, allowed the chaotic rumble of her emotions to fill every empty place inside me. She was beautiful. Courageous. Passionate. Lust roared through her as it did me, and I knew her link to me would enhance her desire until her need matched mine. Her emotions moved through me in a sensual slide inside my mind. She was soft, feminine, loving, even in her thoughts. Gentle. Vulnerable. Unsure.

That last feeling was not one I liked. Not only did I need the males in this battlegroup to know she belonged to someone, I needed *her* to know that truth as well. She was mine. My match. My mate. No one else could have her. The collar proved my claim, even though the colors did not yet match. They would. I would do whatever was necessary to secure and protect what was mine.

The sight of that black band around her throat brought me great satisfaction, bordering on physical pleasure. I sighed, relaxed almost. She belonged to me now and no one else could, or would, ever have her.

She gasped and her eyes flared wide. "You're... glad I'm here."

I smiled. "Yes, mate. Very glad."

"How do I know that?"

"The collars, they connect us."

Her hand lifted to her own neck, her small fingers sliding along the smooth surface. "I'd heard about the collars, about Prillon life, from the warden on Trion. She said Prillons mate in pairs. That I would have two mates."

"I am now and forever your primary male." I paused. "But, the warden on Trion was correct. You shall have two warriors to adore and protect you."

Desire spike through the collar and I nearly groaned. Gods, yes, she wanted that as badly as I. With a small frown, she looked about. "Who is my other mate?"

"I was not expecting your arrival and currently, I do not have a second. I did, but I released him from his oath to me."

She looked down and I felt her sadness. Disappointment. Guilt? Her desire wilted like it had never been, replaced by a painful darkness that was not acceptable to me. "Because of me?"

I tipped her chin up, made her look me in the eyes. "No, mate. You are perfect in every way. Sensual. Beautiful. I am honored to be yours. I released Nevo from his oath several years ago. I tested a long time ago and had lost hope I'd be matched. He was asked to be a second by a fellow warrior who had been mated. His second was killed by the Hive. He didn't wish to leave his female unprotected should something happen to him, so he asked Nevo to join their family. It is an honor to be trusted as a second, to protect and love a female. For Nevo, it was a chance to have the family he longed for. I released him from our agreement."

"So, do you not want a second?"

I sensed her disappointment, knew she was most likely well matched, at least to Prillon, if she truly needed two mates.

"Do not fear, mate. I will take care of you, including finding a second so you are never left alone. I will find one worthy of you. Of us, as a family."

I felt peace sweep through her. Contentment. The ability to ease her mind made me feel powerful and fueled my need for control. Yes, she needed my order. She needed the security I would provide. "You are mine now, Miranda. I will not let you go, unless you demand it of me in the next thirty days."

"Until then?" she asked, shifting her hips and pressing into my hard cock.

"Until then, we can learn each other. I would like to kiss you." I did. Desperately.

"Yes."

I leaned down, tasted her for the first time. Her lips were soft. Plush. A little breathy gasp escaped her throat, and the sound made me eager for more. So I took. Plundered. Ravaged, all the while she was upon my lap.

She was mine. Before the day was through, she'd know it in all ways.

Oh yes, it seemed having a mate was better than I ever imagined.

"I am desperate for you. We must fuck now."

Instead of dropping the blanket to the floor, she stared at me, then burst out laughing.

I arched a brow. "What is humorous?"

"No foreplay? Just... get it on?" She glanced down at the

front of my uniform pants. "You're ready, obviously. Don't you want to see if I'm wet? Eager?"

The thought of her pussy slick with her need for me made me even harder. She was correct. I *was* ready. Just seeing her naked on the transport pad had made me want to drop to my knees and fuck her then and there. But the transport tech was not my second, and I would not share the sight of her desire, the sound of her pleasure, with anyone but my second or those chosen to honor our mating ceremony.

"You are ready."

She bit her lip as she slid from my lap to stand before me, the blanket wrapped protectively around her body. The tilt of her lips made it obvious she was trying to smother a smile. "I am ready because you dictate it or because you are sure I am wet?"

I wanted to sigh, but remembered she was a primitive Earth female. "Because we were matched with almost perfect accuracy. You would not be my mate if you weren't eager to be taken the way I want to take you."

She cocked her head, eyed me. "That actually makes sense." She dropped the blanket so it pooled around her bare feet.

Ah, a bold mate. My cock loved it.

"And how do you want to take me?"

"I want to be deep inside you when you come. I want to make you scream."

She shivered and licked her lips as if she needed another taste of me. She said something else. I didn't hear a word of it.

Holy fuck. She was lovely. Beautiful. Incredible. Pre-cum seeped from my cock just looking at her. Her dark locks fell over her shoulders, her hair so long that it fell to the tips of her breasts. The nipples there hardened before my eyes into tight pink peaks. They were full and lush, more than ample to slake my lust sucking and laving them. Her waist, while soft and curved, tapered and then flared into wide hips. She was not a small female, but well-padded, perfect for a male to grip onto as he fucked her. Not any male. *Me.* My second as well, whoever the gods fated him to be.

"What?" I asked, when my eyes finally met hers, and I realized she was waiting for me to say something.

"I asked if this is the case for every matched mate?"

I shrugged. "I do not care about others. Only you. Your needs are mine now. You need to be touched, and it is my job to do that. You need to come and your pleasure belongs to me."

"What about your pleasure? Is it mine?"

"Yours, mate. As I am yours." Fuck, I would come just standing here before her. I walked toward her, took her hand and led her into the bedroom. If we were going to talk, we could do it lying down. With her beneath me. Or with my head between her thighs.

If I had already chosen a second, we would both take care of her, use two mouths to arouse her, four hands to seduce, two cocks to fuck. Until then, I had her all to myself. I would give her myself in every way she needed. I paused, *felt* her. "Yes. Can you sense my answer? The collar about your neck connects our thoughts. I sense your desire. Your need. Can you not feel mine?"

Her hand went to the black collar, her small fingertips tracing the solid black line where it rested against her skin. Just seeing it about her neck set off a flare of possessiveness I never before imagined. Mine. This female was mine. If I were this eager for her now, what would I feel, *how would I handle* the feelings once my desire was echoed by my second? When we both ached to be with her. Fill her. Fuck her. Care for her?

"That's from the collars? I thought... I mean, wow. Yeah, I can feel your need. God, that's intense. It makes me... hotter."

It was my turn to grin. "Yes, mate. That is how it is. How it *will* be. My need feeds yours, and in turn, yours feeds mine. I can sense your mood. Happiness. Sadness. Pain. Need. It is all there to be shared between us."

"No doubts. No lies," she added.

"None. I give you everything I am, female. And I demand the same from you." I stood now, rising to stand before her naked body and touch what was mine. "You are mine. I will not tolerate secrets between us. I do not play games. I am a warrior of honor, and you are my mate."

The declaration flared between us, the collars turning my simple statement into a feedback loop of surprising intensity. My female had needed to hear those words, needed them with a raging hunger I had not anticipated.

If it was reassurance she needed, I was more than happy to oblige. She would never doubt me, or my desire for her.

Turning both of us so that her back was to the bed, I gave her a gentle push between her breasts so that she fell back onto soft bedding. I dropped to my knees, and with my palms, opened her knees. Wider, then wider still. I could see her pussy now, the pink flesh that *was* wet for me. I felt her burst of arousal at being handled roughly. At me taking possession.

Gripping her slim ankles, I lifted her feet so they rested on the edge of the bed, splayed wide.

Leaning forward, I licked up her slit. She was too far away. Growling, I tugged her hips to the edge. "There. Now I can eat your pussy."

"Trist!" she cried. "We've... god, we just met."

I looked up her naked body and met her startled gaze. Her head was lifted so she could look at me. She tugged at my hold on her ankles, but not to escape. I didn't sense any fear or panic. Only need. Surprise. Longing.

"Yes, and I am going to *meet* your pussy right now. With my mouth."

I didn't say more, only settled between her thighs. Licked her from puckered asshole to clit. Her hands went to my hair, tangled. Tugged. Her need went from a simmer to an inferno within seconds. Her hips shifted and rolled against my mouth. I settled one hand across her belly, pinning her in place. With the other, I slipped a finger inside her. Tight. Hot. Wet. Perfect. I worked her, listening to her sounds to see what she liked. Felt her tremors when I flicked her clit, when I curled my finger over a specific spot inside her.

"Trist... holy shit."

I grinned against her swollen flesh, breathed in her musky scent. I felt her through the collars, knew how she smelled, how she tasted, and I could sense how she liked to get off. She was mine to learn, to play like an instrument.

I gently licked her pussy as I reached down, opened my pants and pulled my aching cock free. It was too big for the snug confines. Pre-cum dripped onto my fingers, and I thrust my hips, eager to fill her. I would give her my seed. All of it, but she would come first.

"You will come, mate. Now."

I went back to sucking and playing with her clit.

"You are so bossy, telling me when to..."

I interrupted with a soft swat to her inner thigh and deepened my voice to the one I used during the middle of an intense battle, the voice hardened warriors didn't dare defy. Neither would she. "Now."

With a wild cry, her pussy fluttered and squeezed my fingers as she let go. I shared the intense pleasure of her release through my collar. I'd never felt anything like it, the connection we shared because we were mates. It made me come as well, thick cum spurting from me, landing on the floor between my knees. I didn't care. I was proud of the fact my mate could make me lose control. But even after my balls emptied, I was still hard, still ready to take her. I would not be satisfied until I filled her completely. Gods, I would not be satisfied... ever.

"Captain Trist." The deep voice came through my quarter's comms system directly following the notification bell.

"What?" I growled, my voice loud and harsh. I'd just come, my face was directly between my sweaty and sated mate's thighs and I was being commed.

"Captain, you are wanted on the command deck."

The voice was one I knew well, a support officer in the engineering department. I felt Miranda's body tense beneath my palm where it rested on her belly. She looked down at me and I was angry. I felt her confusion, her sense of... resignation.

Unless Commander Zakar himself started pounding on the door to my private quarters, the rest of the ship could take care of itself until I'd seen to my mate. I was busy. Very, very busy. "I am with my mate. Tell your superior I am occupied and that she should consider me unavailable until I inform her otherwise. That goes for the rest of the crew as well."

There was a pause. "Understood." The notification bell sounded again, letting me know the call was over.

"Don't you... don't you have to go?"

"Go where?" I stood then and she came up onto her elbows. Looked up at me. Gods, she was gorgeous, a pink blush went from her cheeks all the way down across her breasts. She looked well-sated, but disappointed. In my skill? In the pleasure I gave her? That would not do. I would not allow her out of my bed until she was completely satisfied.

"Don't you have to help run the ship? You're an officer. Don't they need you?" Her small frown of confusion was adorable. Vulnerable. I felt the uncertainty in her, the aching hurt, the fear that I would cause her pain in some way. That was unacceptable.

"Not as much as I need you, mate." I toed off my boots, then stripped, throwing my uniform on the floor without care where anything landed.

"Aren't you going to go? What if something goes wrong? Don't you have a duty to everyone on the ship?"

The emotional turmoil blasting me through the collar caused an ache in my chest that would not go away. Not my pain. Hers.

What idiot had made her feel this way? As if she were not a priority? As if I would have any duty beyond caring for her. I would serve on this ship. I would fight the Hive. But where I'd been fighting for my people before, now I would fight for her. Kill for her. "My only duty is to you, Miranda. You are mine now. You wear my collar. I will fight for you. Kill for you. Die to protect you. So, go? Leave you naked and vulnerable in my bed because someone wants me to look over engine maintenance updates? Absolutely not. My priority is you. The moment you accepted my claim, mate, you became the most important thing in my world." I flicked my gaze to her dripping, swollen pussy. "You, mate, and sating this very greedy pussy."

I sensed all her worries slip away and felt... surprise. Yet I knew she needed to hear it again. And again. "Nothing is more important to me than you are, mate. Nothing."

Lowering my lips to the top of her foot, I kissed her there. Then on her calf. The inside of her knee. Her thigh. Her skin every bit as soft as I'd ever imagined.

"Trist." She said my name and I growled, sucking her clit into my mouth, claiming her again. Gods, she tasted like the sweetest nectar. Mine. She was mine. And nothing would tear me away from this moment, from tasting her, touching her, fucking her. Filling her with my seed.

Her fingers wrapped in my hair, pulling with a sharp sting that drove me wild. She arched her back and moaned as her desire flooded me.

Desire. Lust. Need. An agony of arousal I had given her.

But beyond that, the subtle pain lingered like a ghost haunting her mind, a ghost I was determined to slay. She was mine now, and no one would ever hurt her again.

6

Miranda

STARING up at my new mate, I couldn't believe this was really happening to me. He'd just told off the entire ship. For me. Stripped naked, shed the uniform of the Coalition to be mine. He couldn't go save the world naked.

I couldn't believe he was mine. Really, truly mine. I'd met him less than an hour ago, and yet I knew he was wholly devoted to me. The completely insane psychic link between us through the collars was like some kind of miracle. I could *feel* what he was feeling. Knew he meant every word he said. Knew exactly how much he desired me.

Only me. The truth of it was undeniable and I'd never felt anything like it before. No one had ever wanted me the way he did. No one. Not even...

No. I wasn't going to think about *him*. Not now, with this beautiful Prillon captain between my thighs.

And god help me, he was *gorgeous*. Tall and golden and

pure muscle on top of muscle. He looked like what he was, a warrior. An alien, with his sharp features and intense eyes. But that intensity made my body burn like it never had before. And it was all focused on me. On my pussy. *Oh shit.*

What would I do when there were two mates looking at me like that? Needing me. Wanting me and touching me and fucking me.

I nearly came again just thinking about it. I could wait. Trist Treval, captain and Prillon warrior, was more than enough for me right now. His emotions were drowning me... in the best way possible.

Was this what Natalie felt like with Roark? The center of his world. His everything? She didn't have a collar to sense his emotions, but it was obvious every time I caught a glimpse of him looking at her. Of course, they'd gone through so much, being separated when she'd been transported back to Earth, thinking he was dead. Their bond had been tested... and held.

Trist kissed my foot and my thoughts went back to him, to the lightest of touches. He'd kissed *my foot.* Then my leg. He was working his way back up my body toward my greedy pussy—it was totally fucking greedy for the big cock of his —and I knew where he was going, exactly what he was going to do. He was going to lick and suck me into his mouth and make me come, make me beg and whimper and surrender to him in every way.

I wanted him to dominate me, *need* me, demand I give him everything. I knew I was different from other women in that way, but I needed him to leave me breathless and sweaty and completely at his mercy. I *needed.* Desperately, almost as desperately as I needed to fight the urge to cry. *This* was why I'd become an Interstellar Bride. The devotion I felt from him through the collar, the fierce protective and possessive instincts. The possessive way his hands moved over my skin, the way his mouth clamped down without pause or pretense.

The way Brax had taken me.

Damn it, there he was again. But I shoved the thought away and focused on the golden color of Trist's hair between my thighs. I reached out, ran my fingers through the silky strands. When his tongue did some magical swirl, I tugged, held him in place as I lifted my hips.

My body was all he ever wanted. When Trist said I was his priority, he meant it. When he said he'd fight for me, kill for me and *die* for me, he meant every damn word. I could *feel* his resolve as his mouth closed over me, as his fingers slipped inside my pussy and pushed me to come. He *needed* that from me, to know he could pleasure me, to be the one to provide everything, including orgasms.

I arched off the bed, unable to control the needy sounds coming from my throat as he found my G-spot, then curled his fingers.

"Trist." I said his name, reminded myself that this was Trist, not Brax. My *mate.* He was mine. Really mine. His body was mine. His cock was mine. His heart would be mine, as well.

This total devotion from a mate was what I wanted, what I had been missing on Trion. Trist was everything I wanted. Why did I keep reminding myself of this?

And why did it hurt?

He growled and lifted his head, kissing his way up my body and leaving a sticky trail of my arousal along the way until he hovered over me, his huge cock pressing firmly against the opening of my wet pussy. When I thought he would push forward, he stopped instead, leaning over me. I looked up into his golden eyes and became paralyzed by the raw devotion I saw there. I rocked my hips and the head of his cock stroked over my folds.

God, these Prillon collars were intense. There would be no hiding anything from him. Not my fear. Not my need. My desire. One day, I hoped, my love.

As if he read the thought in my mind, his face softened. "I feel the pain inside you, Miranda. You're here now, with me. I shall ease it. It is my duty. My privilege to make it go away. I shall do anything to see you happy. I vow that you will never need to feel it again. Not with me."

That was it. I couldn't stop the dam of tears I'd been holding back and they slid down my cheeks. He blurred and I blinked, trying to will them away. "I'm sorry. I need you. I didn't mean to make you feel—"

His lips cut off my protest and I lost myself in the gentle exploration for long minutes. When I was a melted pile of goo, when my hands were gripping his tight ass and trying to get him to fill my aching pussy with his hard length, he pulled back and looked into my eyes once more. He would not go in, not yet, and in that moment, I realized, he was in charge. "You are mine, Miranda. Mine to protect. Mine to care for. I will hear about your past, mate. I will hear all of it. I will know what causes this pain."

I shook my head until he kissed me again and I knew through our collar connection that he was holding back, that his body, this restraint, was causing *him* physical pain. I hurt so *he* hurt. His control was like a deep, dark pool of ice water inside him. He would not budge on this. He would demand I surrender every truth about myself. And his resolve soothed something in me I hadn't understood was ragged.

In that moment, I knew his oath to me was unbreakable. One hour in and I was his and he was mine. All I had to do was say yes, accept his claim. The control, his unbreakable will, would surround and protect me. Always.

"I am yours, Trist," I breathed. "Your mate. And you are mine."

His body tensed and I felt the shift in his emotions at my declaration. He'd been like ice a moment ago. Now I felt an explosion building within his mind, a break in his control, not because he was weak, but because I needed him to take me. To be wild. To fuck me until I couldn't remember my own name. "All of you, mate. Body and mind. I will not accept less."

"What about my heart?" I asked, lifting a hand to run a fingertip down his cheek.

He tilted his head and kissed my palm. "That I will earn, but I shall have it."

For a badass alien warrior, he was cute, in an apex predator kind of way. I told him so.

"I am not cute, mate." With a grin that was borderline evil, he thrust forward. Slowly. Stopped halfway in me, enough to be stretched wide about him, opening for him, but not enough to be satisfied. *No. No. No. Don't stop.*

He hovered, watching my face as he filled me, studying me, my reaction. I felt like he was learning me, learning what I liked, what I wanted.

But it wasn't enough to have him opening me up, having my walls ripple and clench about him, trying to pull him deeper. I needed to feel like I was giving him everything. I couldn't explain it, didn't understand myself enough to ask him to do anything differently, so I lifted my arms above my head and held them there, exposing myself to him in every way. Giving myself over to him.

His eyes flared with understanding, and with one hard

thrust, he filled me to the breaking point, the tip of his cock hitting deep inside me.

My head tipped back and I gasped. "Trist!"

My entire body shifted on the bed, my full breasts jiggled as the force of his thrusting moved me up and down on the bed. I did not move my arms. I let him have me, let him give me what he wanted, let him learn and sense what I needed on his own.

Harder. Deeper. I was on the edge and he held himself over me, watching me like a predator. I felt his pleasure, his admiration. He thought I was beautiful and wonderful. Exotic. I could feel his desire through the collar, just as he could probably feel my frustration. My need to come.

I was on the edge, riding the line to an orgasm, but it wasn't enough. I needed... more. I writhed and panted, shifted and clenched my hands into fists.

"Tell me what you need, mate." His order was half growl.

How could I tell him that I wanted him to be bossy, demanding? That my body was waiting for him to give permission for my release? That I wanted him to hold me down and spank me and put clamps on my nipples and my clit? How was I supposed to tell him that now? It was too much to throw down on our first time together. And when he had chosen a second, I was hoping it wouldn't be an issue. Two hot mates. Two cocks fucking me and filling me.

The thought of riding two mates, taking them both at the same time, filled my mind and my body responded, getting wetter around him, one step closer. Just not. Quite. There.

"Ahhh." The sound was half mindless need and half frustration on my part.

"Gods be damned, you *will* tell me what you need." He grabbed my wrists, one in each of his large hands, and splayed them wide above my head in a firm hold. I tried to move them, but I couldn't. He held me down as he stopped moving, cock buried deep. "Now," he growled. "Tell me."

Held down, his cock buried deep but unmoving, commanded to obey, my orgasm ripped through me like an explosion, and I bucked beneath him as his eyes flared wide. A scream tore from my lips at the way I had no choice, no control. The one word, *now,* was a command I'd obeyed. Pinned to the bed by cock and hands, I had no choice. I didn't want one but gave myself to him in that. I needed the comfort, the security of his dominance and power. I could let go, to give him *everything.* I felt his surprise when it was all revealed through the collar, when he felt my orgasm deep inside of him along with the rippling walls of my pussy. His jaw clenched and my pleasure sent him over the edge with me.

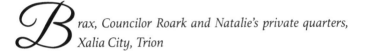

rax, Councilor Roark and Natalie's private quarters, Xalia City, Trion

I IGNORED the bell signal that I would normally use to signify my presence and banged my fist against the door. I didn't care that it was Roark's door, or that he was my superior officer. I didn't care that he was the councilor of the entire Southern continent or whether he might consider my behavior to be rude or disrespectful. I didn't care about anything but him opening the fucking door.

When he didn't answer, I banged some more. Then some more. Harder. If he didn't open the door soon, I'd kick it down.

Finally, it slid open silently and there stood Roark with his new baby girl, Talia, in his arms. He looked ready to kill me, frightening...until you looked at the tiny infant he was holding. She was pure innocence and sweetness, the contrast not lost on me. I felt the same way when I was with Miranda, gentle yet fiercely protective at the same time. The way Roark glared at me was unlike anything I'd ever seen while on duty. His words shocked me more.

"If you've woken Noah from his nap, you will be stunned with my ion pistol until you piss yourself."

Yes, he was deadly serious about my insult in waking his young son.

Well, I was not in the mood to be trifled with, and I needed answers more than I feared Roark and his ion blaster. "Where is Miranda? And who the *fark* is the Coalition soldier currently residing in Miranda's quarters?" He was lucky I hadn't forced my way past him. Only his complete confusion when I mentioned Miranda's name had saved him from a solid beating. He had no idea who Miranda was. None.

Which meant she had moved. Where, I had no idea. But she was mine and I would find her. I didn't care if she'd been transferred to the deserts or the mountains, I would go wherever she was, place my adornments on her and bring her home, to Xalia City, where she belonged. In my bed. In my home. I'd resigned my commission with the Intelligence Core, told Roark that the pirate mess in the south was my last mission. He hadn't questioned my decision. Hadn't asked why. Which I'd taken as his implied consent. He knew I had been in a relationship with Miranda, his mate's best friend from Earth, his son's honorary aunt. Miranda was family to Roark and his mate, which meant the councilor had to know where she had disappeared to. And if Roark didn't know, his mate, Natalie, would.

Roark studied me, quietly rocking his infant in his arms. "That soldier is a delegate from the Northern Hemisphere here for the annual meeting of regional alliances," he said, a dark brow raised. He was not in his usual uniform, but in simple black pants and a gray tunic. The baby in his hold had her mother's fair hair and coloring, but she stared at me with the same dark eyes as Roark's. The fact that she was drooling on her father's arm was plenty of indication she wasn't following anything we were saying. I could let a few *farks* slip out with in front of her, but not her older brother, who repeated every curse word he heard with enthusiasm.

"I don't care where he's from," I countered, full of frustration and sarcasm. "Where is Miranda?"

"Why do you care?" It was not Roark who asked, but Natalie. She came up beside her mate, Noah at her side, the little boy's hair ruffled from sleep. He was holding her hand, his curious eyes staring at me. He knew me, but seemed to be in that stage of needing a little time to orient himself after being rudely awakened before he was ready.

"Should I kill him, mate, for awakening Noah?" Roark asked, staring down at his petite mate.

She shook her head, gave him a small smile. When she turned to look at me, the tender look slipped and was replaced by a less than friendly scowl. "No. He was already awake when the door banging occurred."

Roark sighed and stepped back, allowing me entry, probably realizing I wouldn't be deterred. I offered him a nod of thanks and stepped into their spacious quarters. There were toys strewn on the floor, a child-sized table and chairs beneath a window with the view of the city with a little plate and cup on it. It seemed that was where Noah had his post-nap snack.

"I care because Miranda is mine," I said, turning to face the family of four, but speaking directly to Natalie.

They were a perfect family unit. Roark, strong, powerful and brave, who fiercely protected those he loved. Talia, whom he'd lain down on a blanket on the floor, her little legs pumping in the air. Natalie, who proudly wore his medallion on a chain between her breasts. They were hidden now beneath a soft white top, but many times in the past she'd dressed for formal occasions in gowns with plunging necklines that showed off Roark's emblems adorning her. Noah, who at two, was just like his father, fiercely watching out for the females. He went and stood beside his sister, mimicking Roark's wide-legged stance, as he guarded her. From me. Someone his mother was obviously displeased with.

The corner of my mouth tipped up in pride at the two-year-old. He would grow up to be fierce and brave. I wanted a son to guide and help grow into a strong fighter, who would one day protect a mate of his own.

"Yours?" Natalie shook her head. "Day late and a dollar short, Brax."

"What does that mean?" I understood her words, but the Earth slang was not one I had heard before. A dollar was a form of payment on Earth. Did Natalie expect me to purchase Miranda? That did not make sense and was something an honorable male would never do.

"She's not yours. She never belonged to you," Natalie said breaking me from my thoughts. She sat down with her arms crossed over her chest and a fierce scowl on her face, it was clear she was very angry with me. Her toe tapped on the floor in a fast rhythm that further irritated me.

"Where is she?"

"None of your business." Natalie raised a brow. "And she belongs to someone else now. Someone who will take care of her properly."

Her words clicked and I straightened. Stiffened. "You mean she belongs to that idiot in her quarters? Over my dead body."

Natalie harrumphed. "That can be arranged," she grumbled, turning her attention to the tips of her fingers, which I found odd, until I realized it was a ploy at ignoring me. I was being *dismissed.*

"*Gara*," Roark warned.

"Don't *gara* me, mate. She was nothing to him. Friends with benefits. He had his chance. How long should a girl have to wait?" Natalie refused to look at me, staring down her mate instead. He shrugged and turned to me.

"Friends with benefits?" I asked him. What the *fark* did that mean? Another Earth term I had heard neither Natalie nor Miranda speak.

"Fuck buddies." Her glare was clearly focused on me now. "Friends with benefits. Sex with no strings."

"Strings are dangerous, female. Of course I would not be so irresponsible with Miranda's body."

"You don't get it, Brax. She moved on. You're too late."

"Fuck—" I growled, trying to understand the Earth slang. "Does she belong to that fighter?"

"No, of course not," Natalie snapped, "And watch your mouth in front of my son." She glared at me but softened when Noah sat down beside his sister, who was now fussing, and held her hand. I did not dare point out that she had just used the same word. I was trying to get information out of the female, and she was not cooperating.

Roark came to my rescue. "He took over her quarters after her transport."

My breath caught. "Transport? Where the *fark*—"

Natalie glared.

Where was Miranda? Had she transported to another continent? Gone home to Earth? Who would I have to threaten to get a transport approval to go after her? No one. At least not until I knew where my mate had gone.

"I apologize," I said quickly with a slight bow of my

head, glancing down at Noah. "Where did Natalie go? Where is she now?"

"A battleship in Sector 17," Roark offered.

Sector 17? Why would she go there? Nothing made sense. I frowned, ran my hand through my hair. "I don't understand. That's in the middle of the war with the Hive. Why did you send her there?" I asked Roark.

"Because you didn't want her," Natalie said. "You didn't want her for your mate, so she found a worthy male who did."

"What are you talking about?" That made no sense. "She is mine. Of course I want her. She is my mate."

Natalie tilted her head and there was not a hint of deceit in her gaze. "No. She's not. She was bride tested. She was matched to a Prillon warrior in Sector 17. She's his mate now. I was there when she transported."

Fark. Fark! "When?"

"Yesterday."

"Tell me this is a jest."

Natalie narrowed her gaze even more. I looked to Roark. He wasn't smiling at all.

Talia fussed and Noah popped up, ran over to his mother and tugged her back to the baby so she could take care of her. Natalie scooped the baby up and returned to the couch where she tucked the infant beneath her loose shirt to nurse.

Roark went over, lifted Noah up and grinned at him, patted his little back. "Good job, son. I'm proud of how you take care of your females." Noah grinned at his father, then hugged his neck with his chubby little arms. Roark set him down and ruffled his hair before the boy ran off to the small table to eat his snack.

"Miranda was matched to a Prillon warrior?" How? How was this possible? "But... she's mine!"

Noah looked up from his food and stared at me wide-eyed. I was not used to tempering my emotions for children and this was a difficult time to do so. My female had been matched. To someone else. On a battleship. Light years away.

"You didn't want her. She was tired of waiting," Natalie offered as explanation.

"Didn't want her? Of course, I did."

"You didn't ask her to be your mate."

"She never wanted to be one. She always said she wanted casual. Easy."

"Yes, well, you're an idiot."

Noah giggled and Natalie smiled at him.

I rolled my eyes.

"Haven't you learned yet that when an Earth woman says one thing, she means another?" Roark asked.

"Hey!" Natalie scolded. "That's not true." When Roark gave her a look I didn't understand, she added. "That's not true, all the time."

"You're telling me she wanted to be my mate all along and never told me?"

I ran my hand over my head again, tugged at my hair. She had been mine, in my bed, beneath me. She'd called out my name in pleasure, begged for me, for my cock. But never once had she said she wanted to be my mate. She'd wanted me and yet... she belonged to another.

"You never told her you wanted her to be yours," Natalie countered.

I hadn't. Not once. I'd even told her the last time, in the swing while my cock was deep in her, that someday she'd find a mate who would adorn her as she should be. I hadn't said it was me. *Fark*, at that time, I hadn't realized I wanted it to be me.

But I did now.

"I came back this time to tell her."

"She asked you before you left on this mission to the south. She asked you if you were ready to take a mate." Natalie scoffed. "You even talked about how beautiful she would look when some *other male,* her *future mate,* adorned her."

Gods be damned. I had. The conversation played back in my mind. She'd closed her eyes, and I'd been too distracted by her body to truly pay attention to her needs. I'd misread her. Failed as her male.

"Do you females discuss every intimate moment? That conversation was private."

"Yes, we talk with our best friends. I love her. She's like my sister. And you broke her heart."

"That was not my intention—"

Natalie interrupted me; apparently she wasn't done driving the dagger into my heart. "You've been back in the city for two days and this is the first time you went looking for her."

"How do you know that?" I was shocked and a bit unnerved by her knowledge of my whereabouts.

"Because that fighter has been in her quarters since just after she transported. You'd have been here sooner if you knocked on her door before now."

That was true.

"I resigned," I said plainly.

Roark nodded, went to sit cross legged on the floor beside his son who sat in the chair at the child's table. They were eye to eye and Roark grabbed a bite of whatever was on the plate and popped it into his mouth. "He did," he offered when it looked as if Natalie didn't believe me. "Resigned. Told me upon his return that he would accept no more missions, that he was going to settle down and take a mate."

Natalie gasped. "Why didn't you tell me?"

Roark shrugged. "What's done was done, mate. You did not consult me when Miranda made the choice to become an Interstellar Bride. I had no knowledge of her decision until she had already transported to Battleship Zakar. What is done cannot be undone." He looked at me, sincere regret in his gaze. "I understand your pain, brother, but she's gone."

"Why didn't you tell her?" Natalie asked. Her voice had softened noticeably, but there was no forgiveness in her gaze, only pity.

"Because I wanted my final mission to be complete. I didn't want to have to leave her again, not for a single day, and I had to leave Trion to debrief with the I.C. I haven't gone to look for her because I wasn't here."

"I'm sorry, Brax. She's mated," she said. "It's a done deal. Once she agreed to the match, there was no going back."

"Like hell," I said. I went to the door, waved my hand over the pad to open it.

"Wait!" she shouted as the door slid open. "Where are you going?"

"To the battleship in Sector 17. She's mine. I shall claim her and bring her home."

"But she's mated to another," Natalie said again.

"I don't care about protocol. She's mine. I won't let her go."

Roark looked at me from where he sat next to his son. "I wish you luck, Brax. But the Prillon warrior who has claimed her with his second may not let you live long enough to convince her to return to Trion."

"She's mine."

The door slid closed before Roark could lodge further protest. I wasn't afraid of the Prillon who had taken what was mine. Miranda was a complex and beautiful female. I knew her, knew her needs. He would know nothing, and I would be sure to prove that to both Miranda and the idiot who thought he could satisfy her better than I.

8

M iranda, Battleship Zakar, Command Deck

COMMANDER GRIGG ZAKAR, Trist's boss, was huge, and a bit scary. I'd have been more worried if not for the equally intense woman who stood beside him. Amanda was human, from home. It had been two years since I'd been to Earth, but it was still *home.* But now, with Trist, even after a short time, I felt like home was with him.

"I'm the first bride ever sent into space from Earth," she said, smiling proudly up at Grigg. I'd gone to Trion with Natalie. I could only imagine how afraid she'd been to do it alone. But having her mate waiting for her after transport... if he were anything like Trist, would have eased her mind right away.

The commander cleared his throat, and while he looked down at Amanda with love in his eyes, his words were a reminder. "To spy on me, mate."

Surprised, I knew my head tilted to the side like a

confused puppy's, but I couldn't help it. "You were a spy?" I asked, looking her over. She wore a pretty long dress in blue and looked nothing like a spy to me, although I had no idea what one looked like.

"CIA," she confirmed. "I was supposed to come out here, steal weapons technology and determine whether or not the Hive were a viable threat."

Holy shit. "What? The Hive a threat to Earth?" I'd heard of the Hive, of course. Everyone out here had, but I'd never seen one. Or been this close to the actual war. "I've never gotten near the fight. I was on Trion." As if that explained it. "I haven't seen one of them. Or been close to a battle. But being on a battleship…"

Trist leaned down, whispered, "We may be on the front lines, but I vow to keep you safe."

Amanda's dark brown eyes grew cloudy and she shuddered. "The Hive, they're evil incarnate, Miranda."

The thought made me a bit queasy until Trist's hand settled around my waist and he pulled me into his side. I noticed Commander Zakar did the same with his mate and she melted into him like she was part of him. So intimate and familiar. Their collars matched, a deep blue, meaning she'd accepted his match and been claimed.

God, these collars were something else. Earth women would sell their souls for this shit, knowing what a man was really thinking and feeling? No hiding anything. No lies. Trist hid nothing from me, not his protectiveness, or his desire. He wanted me, and he was making sure I knew it every second of every day. I had to wonder if there was a difference, something even more intense, once the color matched.

Reaching up, I rubbed mine where it rested against my skin. It didn't feel like a collar, not like I'd ever thought of them. A choker, something that cut off some of my air. Stifling, even. But this one felt like it was part of me, part of my skin. Like it had melted into my flesh and become part of me—the way Trist was beginning to feel. Like we were becoming one.

Amanda—Lady Zakar—laughed and the sound reminded me of home. "It's crazy, isn't it?" she asked, catching my eye and waggling her eyebrows. I knew exactly what she meant.

"Insane. Women would kill for this back home," I said my thoughts aloud.

"I know, right?" She grinned.

The commander looked at me, his gaze focused. "Women should not kill anything. What are you referring to, Lady Treval?"

Lady Treval?

Holy shit. I was *Lady Treval*? And I realized, as I noticed every single member of the crew on the command deck trying to eavesdrop, that I was standing here speaking to the commander of the *entire* battlegroup, that my mate was second in command. Like the Vice President of the entire area of space.

Trist had given me a little lesson in battleship roles, so I wasn't totally clueless, thank god. He'd even said that Lady Zakar was the highest-ranking officer on the civilian side. A big responsibility, especially since I got an idea of how large this ship was as we'd walked from Trist's quarters to the command deck. And this was one ship of many.

Did that mean I was second in charge of all of the day-to-day living arrangements out here? What was I supposed to do? I wasn't suited to be a leader. Sure, I was bossy as much as everyone else, but not like Trist. No way. I loved my teaching job. Did they even have teachers out here?

Schools? Surely, they had schools. What did a school even look like on a spaceship?

Amanda giggled and patted Grigg's arm. "Earth slang, mate."

He replied with a little nod as if that explained it all. Perhaps it did, for not everything translated with the NPUs. Even a big, powerful Prillon couldn't understand everything. Perhaps that was why she'd said it, to confuse her mate every once in a while?

I bit my lip and tried not to smile. I was shocked and very, very happy to find out I liked Amanda very much. I would have a friend here. Trist and the commander had been serving together for over ten years, or so Trist had said. I missed Natalie and was relieved to find a woman from Earth all the way out here in space. We weren't from the same hometown, hadn't gone to the same high school, but being in Sector 17 of space, even knowing she was an Earth girl made her feel like my new best friend.

At least she would know the difference between Thor and Spiderman *and* be able to talk chocolate with me. Trist nudged me. "What?"

"The commander asked you a question, mate." He grinned down at me, so I knew I wasn't in too much trouble, perhaps because he could feel my happiness at finding a friend bubbling through my veins like fizzy water.

Question? Crap. I could *not* remember what he had asked me. I hadn't even heard it I'd been so lost in my thoughts.

Amanda patted Grigg's arm again and took pity on me and answered. "The collars. We were saying, mate, in slang, that many women back on Earth would be willing to kill to get their hands on Prillon mating collars."

One of the officers I hadn't noticed before leaned back in

his seat and caught my eye as he spoke for the first time. "Give me the coordinates, Commander, and I shall set course for Earth at once. We wouldn't want any females to suffer when we have an abundance of males willing to collar and claim them rather than waiting for their brides."

The commander now understood I was joking, but obviously the officer hadn't. Commander Zakar shook his head and frowned at his mate. "You're starting trouble on purpose."

She winked at me, so I knew not to worry.

"Don't worry, Grigg, you can spank me later for misbehaving."

Her words shocked me and made me hot. She *wanted* a spanking from her mate. Wanted to be dominated by him. I squeezed my thighs together, felt them slick with my arousal and Trist's seed.

Grigg's eyes darkened at once as he buried his hand in her hair and gently tilted her head up to his, the officer forgotten. "Don't think I won't, female."

She laughed and tilted her head into his touch. "Promises, promises."

He growled and I averted my gaze as—well—I didn't really need to notice the bulge forming in his pants. And the idea of that spanking? Not Grigg giving me one, but Trist, his big hand on my upturned ass. Maybe I was on all fours, maybe I was bent over his knees. A desk, or even standing with my hands against a wall. God. So damn hot.

And in that moment, the collar worked against me. Or for me. I hadn't decided yet when Trist leaned down to whisper in my ear. "I can feel how the idea excites you, mate. A desire I shall explore later." His hand came down, cupped my ass and gave it a quick squeeze.

"Commander, we have a problem."

The swift and efficient voice broke the playful mood in the room and Commander Zakar walked to the officer who had called him. Soon he was bent over a screen in deep discussion with the two officers closest to him.

Amanda gave me a quick hug. "I'm out. I have a ton of work to do, but I can't even tell you how excited I am to have a friend from home here now."

I smiled. "Me, too."

"We'll catch up soon, okay?"

I nodded and she called out her farewells and left the deck. Trist pulled me toward an out of the way corner as the business of running a command ship resumed around us. Despite the serious atmosphere—I *was* standing on the deck of a battleship in outer space—my breath caught in my throat as he squeezed my hip, sliding his palm just a bit lower to cover my ass where no one could see.

"Trist," I breathed, wiggling my hips.

He set his forearm on the wall by my head and leaned down so we were eye to eye. "Careful, mate, or we'll have a challenge right here on the command deck."

That startled me out of my lusty stupor. Trist was dangerous... in a *very* good way. All he had to do was pet me and I froze. More like melted. He was too safe. I didn't keep my guard up, didn't hold my emotions back. I didn't feel like I had to worry about him leaving me, and so I didn't try to be something I wasn't. Didn't try to hide how I felt, as if that were even possible with him. I *was* lonely. Or had been. And lusty. I still was. And happy to belong to someone for the first time in my life. "I'm not doing anything."

He chuckled and his lips grazed my ear. "Look around, mate. Every unmated male on this command deck has their eyes on you. The poor ensign there is going to lose his if he doesn't remove them from your breasts."

I gasped, my gaze flying back to the young male who'd spoken to me moments ago only to discover that my mate spoke the truth. The Prillon *was* staring. At me. And when I looked at him, he didn't look away. No, he met my gaze and held it, hiding nothing of his desire. His free hand drifted down to his cock and he rotated his stance to give me a full-frontal view of everything he had to offer beneath his uniform. "Oh. I don't..." Shit.

I turned to Trist and used his large body to hide the bright red blush I could feel creeping over my face. "I don't know what to do. I didn't mean to do that, I mean, I'm with you and I would *never*—" I didn't want to offend him or have him think I was trying to pick up other guys. I'd done nothing and these fighters were bold. Was this normal behavior on a battleship? In a war zone? Good Lord.

"He wants you," Trist stated plainly.

Well, that was obvious. "But, I don't understand. Are they behaving that way to disrespect you? It's kind of an asshole thing to do."

"Word has spread that I was matched. It's not a common occurrence. Neither is a Prillon not having a second. They want the job. They want to be your second."

My eyes widened. "I thought you would choose your second. That once I wore your collar, no one would bother me."

He lifted a hand to cup my face. "There are many worthy warriors here. He is one of them. As I have no second, many will attempt to gain your attention. It is not an offense to me if they are bold. It would please me to make sure you are happy with the choice. As long as the male you choose is a worthy warrior and protector, I would be honored to accept him as a second."

"That guy just grabbed his cock through his pants, showed me he was hard for me. That doesn't bother you?"

"It bothers you?" His light gaze roamed over my face, paused as if he were *feeling* my answer.

I wasn't interested in the warrior. I wasn't interested in anyone on the spaceship but Trist. But this was new. I was with one mate and I got to pick out a second one? In front of him? I felt like a swinger. "I'm supposed to choose?"

Panic welled up from nowhere and I couldn't get any air into my lungs. That was too much. I didn't want that. That wasn't why I was here. His arms came around me even as my head shook violently. "No. I don't want to. I don't know any of them. I'm sure the warrior over there is nice and all, but no. I don't..." The fresh wounds inflicted by Brax rose within me like lava burning my insides to ash. "I'm not good at choosing men, Trist. The men I choose always hurt me. That's why I went through the Brides Program."

Anger rose within him at my words as did a protective rage that—rather than make me fear him—made me melt into his arms. His hand stroked my hair as he settled me against him. His hand moved from my ass to the small of my back to hold me close. "Hush, mate. I will take care of it. I will choose a worthy male to be your second."

The moment the words left his mouth, I relaxed in relief. Thank god. I didn't want that kind of pressure. I didn't *know* any of these warriors. I'd never met any aliens, other than on Trion, and that hardly counted. Yes, the Trions were bigger than humans and kinky as hell, but they didn't have tentacles or purple penises or weird limbs. Not that Trist did either. But aliens in general, were big, hot, dominant men who loved to fuck their women into submission.

Trist and Commander Zakar were the first *alien* aliens I'd spoken to. I barely knew anything about Prillon Prime, or this battleship, or the warriors who served here. I knew Trist was mine and he would protect me. And I held on to that knowledge with a mind-numbing strength I hadn't realized I possessed. He was mine. I didn't want to choose an alien I barely knew as a second mate when Trist had been fighting and serving with these warriors for years. I would trust his judgment. I knew he would take care of me. I could *feel* his resolve, his devotion. His obsessive need to care for me. And it made me feel content for the first time in my life. Safe. Settled. "I don't care who you choose, Trist. I trust your choice. I only care that you are mine."

His low rumble hit me moments before his emotions made me want to clutch at my chest. I'd pleased him. Not simply pleased him, the pain that came to me through the collars was old, an ache within him that I'd somehow broken open.

"I'm sorry. I didn't mean to hurt you."

His arms tightened. "Sometimes things must break before they can heal."

I thought of Brax and knew exactly what he meant.

Commander Zakar stood and turned to Trist. "I'm sorry to interrupt, Captain, but I need you to take a look at this."

Trist nodded and wrapped my hand in his, pulling me along behind him. With the male attention I was getting, I was glad not to be separated from him.

"What is it?"

"We have lost contact with cargo ship 564." A very large male I assumed was one of the Atlan beasts stood next to an officer running some kind of scanner. It didn't look like radar that I'd seen in the movies. More like a three-dimensional, full color projection of the ship and the space all around us—behind a screen. So cool. I'd never seen anything like it.

Trist tensed, his hand tightened on mine and I felt something shoot through the collar before he shut it down, cold, and I felt nothing. "How long?"

The Atlan checked the screen. "Two hours."

Commander Zakar no longer looked like a friendly male, but a warrior ready to rip someone into a dozen pieces and watch them bleed. "And the last scout patrol?"

"Gone, sir. Nothing for the last twenty minutes."

"Gods be damned." Commander Zakar looked at the Atlan. "Get a ReCon team over there, now. Full Atlan contingent for protection." He turned to Trist. "I want every ship in the group reporting in every fifteen minutes. If they are one minute late, I want to know about it."

"Yes, sir." Trist turned to the male who'd been showing me his... equipment. "Send out the order. Fifteen minute checks, no exceptions. I'm taking my mate to our quarters. I'll return shortly."

"Yes, Captain."

Trist turned to me. "I have to take you back. I'm sorry, Miranda. I must work."

The entire command deck was so full of tension I was getting nauseated just standing there. "What's going on?"

"Our people are disappearing," he said simply. "This is the third ship to go silent in the last two days."

I frowned. How did a ship disappear from space? It's not like there was any place for it to hide. "Disappearing? How? That doesn't make sense."

He kissed me quickly on the lips and pulled me into the hallway, explaining as we walked, his pace quick. "The Hive. They have developed some kind of cloaking technology and we can't detect their craft. They must be boarding our ships and taking our people right out from under us."

I hurried alongside him. "That's terrible. I'll get something to eat, take a nap. Read. I'll be fine for as long as they need you."

Our personal quarters weren't far and seconds later my body was pressed to the door. "But I need you." He leaned down and kissed me, hard and fast and so thoroughly my knees gave out. Of course, he caught me, leaned into me more so I had the solid door behind me and his equally strong body at my front. And kissed me again.

"Get your hands off my mate, Prillon."

Trist froze, his back to whoever had spoken. I couldn't see around his huge chest, but I didn't need to. I *knew* that voice.

Brax.

Trist turned and shoved me behind him in the blink of an eye.

"Security, personal quarters. Code seven." Trist's voice had the snap of a whip.

"Wait!" I said, trying to push my way out from behind him. "I know him."

"That's right, she's mine," Brax said, although I had yet to see him.

Trist growled and had Brax pinned against the wall by his neck. Since he was a seven-foot tall Prillon warrior and Brax was... not, his feet didn't touch the floor.

"No! Don't hurt him."

While I was mad at Brax, I didn't want him hurt. I also didn't want Trist to hurt someone because of me. He might be a warrior but he didn't need that on his conscience.

"She's mine," Brax got out, even though his throat was being squeezed hard enough for his face to turn a mottled shade of purple.

"She's mine," Trist countered.

Three warriors ran down the hall, weapons drawn.

Trist looked to me. "I will not kill him, but he will answer to me."

He released his grip and Brax's feet slapped the ground.

"Take him away."

I watched as the security group dragged Brax off, but his gaze was fixed on me. And I didn't need a collar to know the look in his eye. *Mine.*

Oh boy, this was trouble.

rax, Battleship Zakar, Private quarters

I MIGHT AS WELL HAVE BEEN in the brig. These bare, plain quarters were like a prison, for I was locked within. Even if I got the door opened, a Prillon guard was stationed just outside under Captain Trist's orders. Miranda was on this ship, in the captain's personal quarters. And not only was he a gods be damned Prillon, but he was second in command of the entire battle group.

Just my luck. Miranda is matched first to Prillon, but worse, to a hard-ass, uptight, calculating bastard.

Which was, I realized, exactly the kind of male she would respond to. She was a true submissive, heart and soul. The stronger her male, the safer she would feel.

Only now, locked in this fucking room, did I realize the truth of it. I had not given her what she needed when she was mine. But I loved her. I would not give her up. And my lack was one I would not make the mistake of repeating.

The small room was similar to a fighter's quarters on Trion, except the view was different. I'd been on enough missions to be used to battleships, other planets, utilitarian quarters. *Empty* quarters. Being alone had never bothered me. Until now, until I'd pulled my head out of my ass. Now I didn't want to be alone. I wanted to share my space, my life. With Miranda. I'd used her transport coordinates and followed, eager to make her mine.

But when I'd come upon them... kissing, I'd lost it. She was *mine*, not some seven-foot Prillon's. She might have been matched to him, might have been sucking the lips off his face, but she belonged to me. She responded to me, to my touch, my cock. She loved to be adorned and fucked, given a bite of pain to enhance her pleasure. I knew her body. I just hadn't known her heart until it was too late.

It wasn't too late. I slapped my hands against the window, tried to handle my frustration when I had no one to blame but myself.

I thought of the huge fucker, her match. He'd turned and faced me, shielded Miranda with his body, and I had instantly known she was his as well. He'd protect her with his life, had been willing to do so right then and there. But I didn't want Miranda dead. I just wanted her.

I admired his need to keep her safe, respected him for it, but it hadn't been necessary with me. I wouldn't see her harmed. But perhaps I had. Perhaps I'd hurt her in the worst way. Not physically, but emotionally, and he knew that. He had a fucking collar about his neck so that meant he'd at least sensed her reaction to seeing me again, hearing my voice.

I didn't need a collar to know that the gasp I'd heard was full of pain. Surprise. Regret. And I knew by the way she clung to him for reassurance, for safety, that she was his now, too.

He'd instantly called in guards, then tucked Miranda inside his quarters. Yes, he was a protective bastard. By the look on her face, she'd been upset—I wasn't sure if it had been directed at me or for the big guy's bossiness—and hadn't been happy to be left in the quarters. Alone. I'd seen the collar about her neck, noticed it wasn't the same color as his.

He'd leaned down, whispered something in her ear, then kissed her once more. Before my eyes, I saw her soften, bend to his wishes. She glanced at me once and tipped her chin up in that fiery defiance I knew so well, then the door slid shut between us. Yes, she was pissed at me.

The guards had arrived then. Two Prillon warriors, one who Trist had ordered to remain outside of his quarters, the other to follow us down the hallway. Trist hadn't said a word, just pointed and began to walk. If he was leaving Miranda alone, then he was confident she was safe. I might not like him, but I was confident in his protection of his mate.

Fuck, not his mate. *My mate.*

The ion pistol at his hip, and the one the additional guard had held, had been enough to get me moving. I was the outsider here even though it was *my mate* I'd walked away from. I was repeating it over and over in my head because it was true, regardless of the fucked-up situation.

Four hours I'd been stuck. Trapped. Waiting with nothing to do but get angrier and angrier. At myself. Not her. Never her.

I paced, looked out the window at the never-ending expanse of space, the distance that had been between me and Miranda since I'd completely fucked up.

Was he now fucking Miranda? Had he put me here to go back to her, to make her forget me? When I got my hands on him I'd—

The door opened and *he* stepped in.

"You are Valck Brax of Trion. A doctor, but it seems your duties have gone beyond medicine." The Prillon had to be over seven feet tall. He had the angular features of his race, the light coloring. He also had the stiff bearing of a fighter, of one who was always in control, always in command. It was required of those who served on battleships, for they wouldn't handle the emotional toll otherwise.

"Is that what you've been doing all this time, scanning my file?" I countered, crossing my arms over my chest.

"We have lost a cargo ship to the Hive. Your past exploits have not been a high priority."

My shoulders went back at the seriousness of the problem at hand. "Has it been recovered?" I asked. While Miranda was the most important thing in my life, I knew she was safe. He wouldn't be here otherwise. But there were many fighters on a cargo ship. Lives were at stake. I would not diminish their service by being petty.

"No. I would not discuss this with you, but I see you have a top level I.C. clearance."

"I do." This Prillon didn't fuck around. And if he knew my clearance level, his had to be... higher.

"There have been multiple attacks since the loss of Battleship Varsten in Sector 436. For now, we have I.C. operatives and our best science teams working on the problem. I have a few hours to take care of Miranda. It is time for me to focus on my mate and what is best for her."

My jaw clenched when he said the words *my mate*. He emphasized the words and I had no doubt he had done so purposely. Yes, he had her. He was her match. He wore the collar and so did she. While she hadn't made the claim official—I knew she had thirty days to decide—she belonged to him. She was his to protect. His to bed. His to seduce and learn and convince her to accept his claim.

I was the outsider here. I just had to change that. But I had a huge Prillon standing in the way of me somehow making Miranda understand I'd been wrong.

"Shouldn't Miranda be the judge of what's best for her?" I countered, stepping toward him.

"I know what she wants, what she needs. She had entrusted me with her life and her happiness."

I quirked a brow. The laid back, easy going female I knew? The one who'd said she wouldn't keep me from my work, that we were casual and *fuck buddies*? "Has she? The same way she begged me to take her? Touch her? Kiss her?"

"You did nothing but cause her pain. You will not get near her."

"The only way I touched her was for her pleasure." I shouldn't have said the words, knew they were wrong, knew I was being an ass, but I wanted to take a stab at this arrogant warrior who had what was mine. My female. My mate. She was mine. "She loved every minute of it, Prillon. She's mine."

His eyes narrowed and every line in his body tensed. I didn't even have time to blink before his fist connected with my face.

Fuck! I stumbled back, put my hand to my nose. Broken. Blood poured down my chin and onto my shirt. It hurt like hell, but it wasn't going to stop me, nothing a ReGen wand wouldn't fix. But a wand wouldn't fix what I'd broken with Miranda. Only words, actions on my part would heal her.

His breathing was ragged, his fists clenched. "She does not want what you offer. She craves structure. Dominance.

She craves reassurance that she will be valued above all others. She was nothing to you, Trion. She chose to leave you. She chose to come to me."

Every word he said was like a gut punch, the pain worse than a physical blow would have been. True. It was all true. She had chosen to leave me, to find him. To belong to him. That was as direct a punch as the one to my nose. "I had a job to do, a duty to help my people."

He nodded once. "I understand that. Respect it, even. But you placed the needs of others above those of your mate."

"You are correct. That is why I'm here. I've resigned. Walked away from it all. For her. She comes first now."

"Yes, she does," the captain vowed. "But not with you. I will not see her hurt."

"I want to talk with her. Apologize. Remind of her of what we share. What she needs from me."

"She doesn't need anything from you," he snapped. "She has a mate."

"She needs my touch. She craves it. The feel of a clamp on her clit. The shimmer of jewels on her pebbled nipples. The tightness of my bindings about her wrists as I fuck her."

He charged then, but I was expecting him. I pivoted to the side and missed the punch of his right fist, but I was caught by the grab with his left. We slammed into the windows, and I gave him an uppercut to the stomach.

A whoosh of air escaped his lungs, but it did nothing to incapacitate him. He was large, sturdy. Fucking solid. A formidable opponent. Because he was taller, I bent down, charged and wrapped my arms around his legs, tipped him over like a leafy tree on Viken.

He hit the floor with a thud, the small table by the couch

shoved out of the way. A light fixture dropped to the floor with a crash.

On his back, his hand shot up, struck my ribs. "You had her, Brax. She was yours and yet she was so unhappy she left you behind. If you were an honorable male, you would walk away." The words were fierce, but so was my punch. I hit the socket of his eye, my knuckles aching from the strike.

"I'm not fucking honorable. Not when it comes to protecting her."

He hissed, and gritted out, "She is mine. You can't contest the accuracy of the matching protocols. Go back to Trion!"

He pushed me up and off of him. I flew across the room and landed on my ass, but I was instantly back up. I caught my breath, wiped my nose with the back of my hand. The bleeding had lessened to a trickle.

He climbed to his feet and glared at me. "She is mine. She is a Prillon bride. I will choose a second and we will care for her. Go home, doctor. She doesn't belong to you. Not anymore."

I shook my head, spit blood out of my mouth onto the floor. "No. l love her and she loves me. Two days with you didn't change that fact. She *is mine.* Her heart is mine. Her body is mine. This isn't Viken, warrior. I won't share her with two others. She's mine and will go back to Trion with me."

He shook his head. "She will not go to Trion. She is mated to Prillon Prime. To me. She wants two mates. Not three."

"Then where the fuck is your second? Is he with her now? Fucking her as we fight?" I pointed to the door. As if conjuring her up, the door slid open and she appeared.

Behind her were the two guards from earlier, although when she came into the quarters, they remained outside.

She took in the room, the mess we made, my bloody nose, the warrior's eye, which was quickly turning black from the strength of my punch.

"What the hell are you two doing?"

We turned to face her, stood side by side. Fuck, she was more beautiful than I remembered. Her dark hair was long down her back, dark green gown fit her like a glove. Her face, while angry, had a glow to it. She looked soft and flushed, as if she were... content.

"We are fighting," the warrior said.

"Are you going to whip your cocks out next and measure?"

My eyebrows went up at her question. "Do you wish to compare our cocks?"

She gasped, eyes focused on me with utter disgust. Disdain. Rage. And... hurt.

"Mate, look at me," Trist said.

Miranda instantly responded to the command and turned to face him, her gaze softening, her eyes growing glazed with emotions she didn't try to hide from him. Not me. Him.

Fuck.

"I know the question was one of those Earth terms that do not process, but the literal reference is what we understand. Do you wish to compare our cocks?"

He asked the same question as me and I gave him a quick glance. I couldn't read him, but it seemed the two of them were having a conversation through the collars.

Miranda bit her plump lower lip. "No. That's ridiculous. That was the point."

He took a step toward her. "Mate. I feel you, remember

that. I feel your need for him. I also feel the hurt. It's the pain I've sensed all along."

She looked to me, nodded.

"I will kill him."

He might be bigger, but that was not happening.

"Trist, no. I don't want him dead."

"What do you want?" he asked.

"She wants me to adorn her, to give her nipple rings and my medallion to mark her as mine."

Miranda gasped. Trist—that was the fucker's name —growled.

"She is mine, doctor. Take one step closer to her, assert your claim one more time, and I will kill you."

"That would hurt her, Captain. She loves me. She's mine."

Trist turned on his heel, facing me. I expected rage. Passion. A lust to kill. Instead I was met with cold, calculating precision. Ice. He was fucking ice. Unbreakable. Unbendable. Solid.

Miranda glided to his side and slipped her hand in his, whether for her own comfort or to prevent the Prillon from carrying out his threat to end my life, I wasn't sure. But there was no doubt now, she was his. It was in the way she leaned into him, obeyed his commands, the way she looked at him, touched him.

Fuck. A change in strategy was in order...

10

*M*iranda

I COULDN'T BELIEVE what I was seeing. The room, if that's what it could be called after these two had destroyed it, looked like a dumping ground for broken things. The table was smashed, the sofa torn in multiple places. Anything fragile or breakable was in pieces on the floor and both of the males I cared about were bleeding from cuts and scrapes all over their faces, arms and fists.

No doubt, they were hurting and bruised on the inside as well.

Idiots.

I held Trist's hand and leaned into him as the tension faded from the room. This was something I had never imagined happening. Not in a million, billion years. Never. I loved them both. Which sucked, because I could only keep one of them, and with Trist's hand in mine, I knew who I would choose if I had to. His devotion to me, his care, his strength of will is what I needed more than I needed hot sex, nipple clamps and leather straps tying me to the table as Brax fucked me.

Both would be nice. I wasn't one to lie to myself. But that didn't look like it was going to be in the cards for me. And I would be okay with that. I had to be.

"What the hell do you two think you are doing?" I put my hands on my hips, felt the silken softness of the dark green gown beneath my palms. Trist had placed me in this gown earlier this morning. He'd taken his time, washing every inch of me in their strange shower tube, then ordered the dress from the odd black square S-Gen machine in the corner of our bedroom. Everything was different on a battle-ship. Smaller, more compact, except for the Prillon's them-selves. Then everything was bigger, including the size of the room itself. *Our* bedroom. *Our bed.* Something I'd never had with Brax, something I had needed to fill the empty ache inside me. Not the bedroom, duh, but the long-term sharing.

I'd come here, to these guest quarters Brax had been assigned, to explain that to him. I wasn't going back to Trion with him. I still loved him. I couldn't help it. I'd given him my body without reservation and come to respect him as not just a lover, but as an honorable male. He was a doctor and a warrior, but I wasn't ever going to come first with him. I'd made peace with that. Even gotten tested, matched and transported halfway across the galaxy.

The care Trist had shown me since my arrival had gone a long way toward healing the wound Brax had left behind. The gown was soft and every bit as beautiful as anything I would have worn on Trion. I felt like a sex goddess for the first time ever. And it was because of Trist. I was familiar with the S-Gen technology. They had S-Gen on Trion as well, but I'd only ever used the one in the kitchens, and they were smaller, not designed for full body scans. Trist had pointed out that the color of the dress matched his collar, a small detail I had already noticed. In his own way, he was adorning me as a Trion would, marking me as his in front of the others, and I loved it. Loved that he was broadcasting his dedication and connection to me.

Unlike the sober-faced fool from Trion who was crawling onto his hands and knees, attempting to stand. He must have been hurt more than I thought because he had to shake his head a few times before he pulled himself to his feet.

Trist, however, seemed to get an extra surge of wrath. He was on his feet instantly, blocking my view of Brax completely. I had no doubt that Brax wasn't going to get near me unless Trist allowed it. He was protecting me and even though I still had feelings for Brax, that one move, and the fierceness and protective rage I felt through the collar, gave me the confidence I needed to walk to Trist's side and stare down at the male who had broken my heart. Trist was mine now. I still cared for Brax, but Trist had stolen an equal share of my heart, and I wasn't going to give that up. He was mine. Brax would have to deal. He'd had his chance.

"Do not even think about getting near my mate, Trion, or you will need someone to carry you to a ReGen pod."

"She's mine, Prillon. She had no right to sign up for the Brides Program. She shouldn't even be here."

Trist tensed at Brax's words, and I felt the need to attack burning through him. I didn't belong to Brax, but I didn't want him to get hurt either. I placed my hand on Trist's arm and held him still with that one small touch. He was so sensitive to my mood, my needs, that he quieted instantly and looked down at me.

"Don't hurt him, baby," I said. Where the endearment came from, I had no idea, but there it was. Trist was mine. I'd never allowed myself to call Brax anything other than his name...or Master. But that didn't count. And my ex back on Earth? He'd hated pet names. Called them stupid and childish, so seeing a huge Prillon melt at the term made me feel oddly powerful and completely adored. God help me, I was in love with Trist already. He was so strong. So noble. So safe. I let him feel it all and the final bit of anger left him as he stared into my eyes.

"You still care for this male?" Trist asked the question, but there was no hurt coming from him, only confusion. "How? He's the one who hurt you. He's the source of the pain I feel from you, even now." Trist looked from me to Brax and his gaze hardened. "Especially now."

Stepping in front of Trist, I reached for his arm and wrapped it around me so I could lean into his strength as I faced the Trion doctor who'd first mended my soul, then broken my heart. "Yes. I loved him."

Brax opened his mouth to speak, but I held up my hand to stay him. I didn't want to hear what he had to say until I'd explained to my mate.

Even though I looked down at Brax, I spoke to Trist. "I was broken when I left Earth for Trion. The man I was with on Earth was cold and mean-hearted and made me feel small and broken. Doctor Brax helped me heal." I thought of exactly how he'd accomplished that and my body heated. Trist must have felt my desire spike because his constant need for me echoed back through the collars until my nipples pebbled under the gown and my pussy grew swollen and wet. His heat at my back, his scent, made me ache. But there was also Brax, staring at me with *that* look, the look my *master* had given me when he was reading me like a book, when he knew exactly what I needed. What I craved. What would make me whimper and beg and surrender.

"I can feel your desire, mate." Trist leaned down and whispered into my ear. "Is your need for me, mate? Or for him?"

I couldn't lie. "Both."

"Gods be damned." Trist pulled me close so I could feel the hard length of his cock pressed to my back, even as he stared down Brax. "What the fuck am I supposed to do about you, Doctor?"

"She needs me, Trist," he said. "And I had her first."

That made me angry. I wasn't a toy to fight over between two preschoolers. "Shut-up, Brax. I swear to God, if you say another word, I'm going to let Trist tear you to pieces."

Trist kissed my shoulder and I felt his grin. Sensed he was like a little boy who'd just won King of the Hill on the playground even as Brax's eyes darkened with anger. And lust. I knew his looks just as well as he knew mine.

"You *had* me," I told Brax. "Past tense. You had me and made it perfectly clear that I wasn't what you wanted in a mate."

He shook his head, winced. "You're wrong."

"Shut up and listen to me." When both males were quiet, I continued. "I asked you, Brax. I asked you when you were going to be ready to claim a mate. Do you remember what you said?"

He closed his eyes for a second, then looked to me. "Yes, I—"

I interrupted him. "You said you would continue to serve Councilor Roark for as long as you were needed. You also said you could not claim a mate while you served because the job was too dangerous and you would be gone for extended periods of time."

"Yes, but—"

"No." He was *not* going to talk his way out of this. I was right. "You even *adorned* me with *temporary* jewels and told me how good I would look when my future *mate* adorned me permanently."

He sighed. "I know. You are very beautiful, *gara...*"

"*Gara*?" I practically yelled the word. "*Gara!*" I tried to pull free of Trist's hold so I could go beat the crap out of Brax myself, but he held me back without even shifting his feet. Damn it, he was strong. "Don't you *dare* use that word when you speak to me. Not now." That word was reserved for love matches. Mates in truth. Males who both treasured and adorned their mates. Like Roark did for Natalie. I had wanted to hear that word for so long that his use of it now made me freaking *furious.*

Brax said nothing and long minutes passed in silence as I tried to calm down. Trist watched Brax and I wondered if he saw what I did in Brax's eyes.

Regret? Pain? Longing?

Or was all of that just my overactive imagination?

I could barely think for the rage that had exploded inside me, rage I had repressed until now. It covered the hurt, which was great, but I was having trouble breathing.

Brax's normally caramel colored skin faded to a pale yellow and he finally seemed to understand just how much his actions had hurt me. Trist remained silent as Brax dropped to one knee and bowed his head to me. "You are my heart, *gara*. I knew that night, when I adorned your body with green jewels, that I could not live without you."

I was shaking my head in disbelief, but he was staring at my feet, or the floor, or something. I couldn't go anywhere because Trist held me in place. And thank god for that because his solid strength at my back kept me sane. I melted against him and let *my mate* feel my gratitude, my comfort, my complete trust in him. I allowed him to hold me and he allowed me to speak freely. "I don't believe you, Brax. You had six months."

"That was supposed to be my last mission, Miranda. The day you snuck away without saying goodbye was the same day I resigned my commission with both the I.C. and Councilor Roark."

Trist tensed at the mention of the I.C., but I had no idea what that was—so whatever. Something to do with Brax's secret missions, no doubt. But I didn't care. Was past caring.

"I waited for you, Brax. Idiot that I was. I waited more than a month. But you came back to Xalia City and didn't contact me. I hadn't seen you in weeks, and you came and went without one word." That had hurt the most. That had been the moment I truly understood what I meant to him. Nothing.

"I couldn't bear to claim you and then leave your side. Roark knew I was done. The I.C. knew. I needed two days to finish debriefing on Prillon Prime. I was going to ask you to be mine forever when I returned."

Was that possible? The anger drained out of me and all that was left was the pain. But even that information wasn't enough. Not anymore. "Trist is mine, Brax. I underwent testing and was matched to a Prillon warrior. I need him. I want him. I can't go back to Trion, and I don't want to."

At my declaration, Trist's hand splayed over my waist in a blatant show of possession, but I didn't object. It was exactly where I wanted to be... in his arms. Belonging to him.

And if that wasn't enough?

I told that small, irritating voice to be quiet. He wasn't the end of the line for me. No. I would have another mate, another sexy, dominant, alpha mate to love me. To adore me. To actually *want* to be with me. A second. And I *wanted* two warriors. I wanted to be overwhelmed and drowning between two dominant males. The thought made me so hot I could barely function. And I couldn't have that with Brax.

Brax raised his gaze, not to me, to Trist. "And where is your second, Prillon?" Brax looked around the room, making quite an exaggerated show of it. "Shouldn't he be here? Protecting your mate from me?"

"I have not chosen a second." Trist went from relaxed to alert so quickly my mind spun with the rapid switch in his emotions.

Brax held Trist's gaze and rose once more to his feet. "I would be your second."

Trist pulled me back so that I was beside and a bit behind him. "Don't even think about it, Trion. You are a doctor, not a warrior. You are small. Weak. You hurt Miranda. You are not worthy of my mate."

Brax's smile was pained, the deep lines at the corners of his eyes and around his mouth new. "You are correct. She is priceless beyond measure. And I did hurt her, although that was never my intention. I was a fool. I am not worthy of her, Warrior. Neither are you."

Trist grumbled his agreement, but Brax continued.

"I am neither small nor weak. While I am a medical doctor, I am a trained fighter, a former officer in the Coalition Fleet Intelligence Core. I have fought. I have killed. But know this, I would die for her, kill for her..." His gaze drifted to mine. "I would even share her, Captain, if that's what she needs to be happy."

The idea of Brax being my second mate made my head spin and my heart race inside my chest.

Was it possible? What would Trist say? He'd said before

that I could choose a second, but I hadn't wanted to try to choose from a spaceship full of strangers. But Brax wasn't a stranger.

The thought was in my mind now, and I couldn't stop imagining myself naked, adorned and being taken by both of them.

Jeez. Was I actually panting with need? That was embarrassing. I cleared my throat and tried to focus on the conversation the two males were having. I'd missed some of it already, my ears ringing. Was this panic? Shock? Fear? Was I losing my mind? Imagining things? Was this a dream?

My body didn't think so. Everything felt heavy. Heat reached my core and every beat of my heart was sending throbbing pulsations through my wet pussy. I was in pain from want. From *need.*

Brax was talking... "Let me guess, Warrior. You were fucking her, filling her pussy. She was going wild, riding the edge, but just couldn't come. Her orgasm remained out of reach, as if she needed something more."

"Oh, God. Stop talking." I did not want to be here for *this* conversation.

Trist, however, was powerfully interested in what Brax was saying. I felt his confusion, his intense curiosity, through our collars. "Continue, Doctor. Tell me what you know of my mate."

"She needs her lover to take control, take away her indecision. Her guilt. Her doubt. She needs to be set free from the fear of making the wrong choice, of trying to determine what her lover wants or needs. She needs to surrender completely. To submit."

Brax's words made me shiver. Was that how he thought of me? Was I weak? Indecisive?

I thought of my time with Trist, of how he'd pounded

into me, my body on fire. Of how he'd grown frustrated, demanding I tell him what I needed. I couldn't. Only when he'd held me down and told me to come, ordered me to let go, had I been able to ride my orgasm and give myself to him completely.

Brax knew me. It was true. He'd created a monster in me, a monster who needed things I wasn't sure Trist would be comfortable with.

Trist's next words shocked me, but not as much as the smugness coming at me from the collar. "I became aware of my mate's needs last night. I assure you, Doctor, there are many worthy Prillon males on this ship more than capable of satisfying her desire for a dominant male, warriors who would be honored to join me in accepting her submission and surrender." His voice was pure, molten heat. Sex. Raw and untamed.

I clamped my legs together and rubbed my breasts against Trist's side. Were they trying to kill me?

"I want you. I want both of you." The words left me before I thought to censor myself.

Trist turned and looked down at me. I knew he could feel my arousal. I'd never been in this state before, at least not standing in a room, fully clothed. If one of them touched me now, kissed me, brushed against me? I was on the edge already. Ready to come.

Ready to submit to both of them.

Trist lifted a hand to my cheek and stroked me with such gentleness I swayed, ready to rip my clothes off. "You want this? Me? And him?"

I nodded. I did. I still loved Brax. And I loved Trist. This was... well, I'd thought it impossible. But this was my nirvana. Heaven. A dream I'd never dared have imagined for myself. "Yes."

He stared into my eyes for long seconds and I didn't hide anything from him. Not my need, my emotions or my fears —fears that he'd say no, that Brax would leave again, that somehow, I would be hurt. Either way, I could be hurt.

Trist turned his head and looked at Brax, who'd taken a step forward. "You will follow me to our quarters, Doctor. There, we will satisfy my mate together. But you are not my second. You will need to prove yourself worthy, and not just in my mate's bed. Do you understand?"

Brax nodded. "Yes."

I thought Trist was finished, but he added one more warning. "If you hurt her again, I will end you. Do you understand that?"

"I won't. I give you my word." Brax set his hand over his heart.

With Brax's agreement, Trist turned back to me. "I will accept him into our bed for you, mate. Even if he pleases you well, he will have to prove himself to me in battle. Do you understand? He must prove he can protect you as well as pleasure you to be worthy."

I nodded. I understood. This might be a one-time thing. Trist would choose his second. Trist would decide whether or not Brax had proven himself worthy.

And I was fine with that. Trist was my world now, he defined the safe space I reveled in. I surrendered to him in that way, and I was content. "Yes, mate. Thank you. I don't trust myself when it comes to him."

Brax started to protest, but one sharp look from Trist ended it before he got a word out. "You will not speak to her of claiming. Do you understand. She is mine. You will either prove your worth to *me*, or you will return to Trion."

11

*M*iranda

THIS WAS INSANE. This was my dream. This was... reality? Brax really did want me. Enough to come after me halfway across the galaxy. And Trist, he wanted me, too. I'd never been fought over before and while it was completely ridiculous, it was hot as hell. Two guys staking their claim, beating their chests. My ovaries didn't stand a chance. And my vagina?

The way they were both looking at me with heated gazes full of blatant intent, it didn't stand a chance either.

"I brought something for you," Brax said with his deep master voice. I'd called him that before because I had considered him one. But that had been when we were doing the friends with benefits thing. But now, calling him master meant something different. Something... more. I wasn't ready to call him that yet, for I didn't completely trust him. With my body, yes, but my heart?

He'd have to prove himself.

Reaching into Trion uniform pants, he retrieved something, then held out his palm so I could see. I recognized the green gems instantly.

My pussy clenched remembering how they'd bitten into my tender flesh, the sharp feeling morphing into a burst of heat. Morphing into an orgasm so painfully sweet...

Trist growled and stalked over to the wall, leaned against it and crossed his arms. I felt his rage, his possessiveness. He didn't want to share me with Brax, but he would. If he were human, he'd probably hate the knowledge that Brax had been with me first. That we'd had sex for months, that I'd liked it.

But Trist wasn't human. It was in his nature to share a woman. It was an honor to do so. He'd been the one to use that word when he'd spoken of the second he'd had, who'd gone off to join another family.

He wanted me to be with another man. He'd watch me. They'd even take me together. And that made me shiver. That made me hot.

Trist growled again, his glare now filled with heat. His cock was hard in his pants, thick and bulging, not something he intended to hide.

He wanted me. He wanted me hot. And if Brax got me hot, then he'd allow it.

And from where he'd moved, he intended to watch. Close enough to have his own porno, close enough to save me if I needed it, but far enough away to give Brax the room to do what he wanted.

And I wanted. I rubbed my thighs together in anticipation.

Brax grinned. It was the sure, quick smile I was used to with him. Panty melting. Flirtatious. Trist wasn't easygoing enough to offer me a look like that, but it also came with a price. Easygoing in nature and easygoing in a relationship. Or so I'd thought.

"See the chain? It's the one I brought for you, to claim you."

Trist growled a third time.

"Now?"

I'd told Trist he was the one I wanted, that I'd wear his collar, but I wasn't claimed. Our collars didn't match color. I'd been content to wait until he said it was time, for I was content in submitting to his judgment. I knew he'd know when it would be perfect.

But Brax? I wasn't ready for that yet. The fact that he'd brought them with him from Trion, that *he* was ready, spoke volumes.

He shook his head. "I won't claim you now. You have a little less than thirty days, correct?"

I glanced at Trist, then nodded.

"Today you will wear the nipple clamps you liked so much, but I will add the chain. You will show your primary male how beautiful you look when you are adorned."

Trist huffed. "She does not need jewels and gold to be beautiful."

I smiled at him, smiled at the fierce wave of possessiveness I felt through the collars. He wanted me naked. No frills. That got him hot.

But I did like the gems. When I wore them for Brax, I did feel beautiful, in a completely different way than with Trist.

Oh, why did I ever think being with two aliens was hot? It was *hard!* Two bossy, dominant males to make happy, to keep from killing each other. To satisfy. I'd have to get on the comms and talk to Natalie about the realities of multiple mates. Two cocks were one thing, but the rest of them?

Their bossy natures, their fists to fight? Their cranky personalities?

"That is true, she is lovely bare. But bejeweled and begging?" Brax made a little hum sound as he adjusted his cock in his pants.

He held out a hand. "Come here, *gara*."

I glanced at Trist, who remained stoic. Yet, I could sense his approval through the collars even without the slight nod of his head.

I was eager for this. I'd dreamed of this in the testing. It was what I wanted, what I *needed*. Two males, two completely and totally different males, to give me everything.

I took a breath, then walked over to Brax.

Brax

SHE WAS SO BEAUTIFUL. Everything I ever wanted. How had I not seen the way her long hair had hints of red as it caught the light? How had I not seen how small she was, how dainty? Having a mate who was seven-feet tall only accentuated that. I wanted to wrap her in my arms and shelter her. Kiss her. Caress her and tell her how beautiful she was.

I also wanted her on her knees. Submitting. Begging.

There was no doubt Trist was a dominant mate. He was the primary Prillon in their match. There was no second.

There was now. Me.

His dominance was also what Miranda craved. It had to be, for their match was near perfect. It didn't eliminate me, only confirmed I belonged with them. He needed a second; she needed me. I just had to prove I was worthy of her.

Starting now.

When she stood before me, I reached out and cupped her jaw with my palm, stroked my thumb over her cheek. Her eyes fell closed and she tilted her head as I brushed the softest of skin.

She was softer other places, like the curve of her breast, the inside of her thigh. I'd get there.

Eventually.

"Shall we show your Prillon how you look with your nipples clamped? Bedecked in gems?"

She licked her lips, then nodded.

"I need the words, *gara*."

She swallowed, then looked away. "Yes," she whispered.

I didn't need a collar to know what she *wasn't* saying.

My thumb continued to stroke her cheek as I spoke. "It's all right, Miranda. You don't have to say it. Not yet. When you are ready, you will call me Master again."

Her eyes met mine and I saw relief there. Contentment.

My cock pulsed in my pants. I stepped back, dropped my hand. "That dress looks pretty on you, but it will look just as nice on the floor."

Slowly, as if just the delay was a tease to my cock, she lifted her hands to her shoulders, slid the thin straps of her green gown--the color of it did not go unnoticed by me, matching the color of her mate's collar, of her mate's family colors--off her shoulders, then down her arms.

The farther it traveled down her body, the more she showed. Every bit of her beneath was bare. Nothing covered her breasts. No scrap of fabric covered her pussy.

I couldn't help but emit a similar growl from my chest as Trist had. She was a vision unclothed. Full breasts, plump nipples which hardened even as I watched. A slightly rounded belly and full hips. She was not a waif, but lush and thick in all the right places. Perfect to hold, to grip as I fucked her.

That I remembered well.

When the material pooled at her feet, she stood tall and proud, but I saw the touch of nerves in her brown eyes, in the way her fingers moved.

I would not make her wait. Reaching out, I cupped her breast, remembering the delicious weight of it. She sighed and thrust her chest into my palm. She wanted it.

Trist made a deep sound as if he were an Atlan who had a beast within. I afforded him a second of my attention. He had not moved from his spot against the wall, affording him a clear view of our mate.

Yes, ours. I would prove it with every touch.

I could understand him, for I felt as if I were possessed by something. Not a beast, but a need so great, so fierce, I would rage if I could not have what I wanted.

But cupping her breast soothed me. She was here, before me. Whole. She wanted me. Wanted this.

The nipple clamps were connected by the thin golden chain. It was light, only offering the slightest tug on her nipples once clamped. It would be my medallion that not only would signify her as mine, but offer her the constant pull as a reminder of our match.

I held one clamp between my fingers, let the other drop so it dangled by the chain as I worked her nipple with my thumb and forefinger, tugging and pulling gently until it was a stiff peak.

Only then did I lower my head, keeping my gaze on hers the entire time, and take the tip into my mouth. Suck. Lick.

And when she moaned and her fingers lifted to tangle in my hair, I stood back up.

"The first one," I said, opening the clamp and setting it on her bright pink nipple, letting it close, then adjusting the tightness of it.

I watched her eyes, saw the flare of pain as it became snug, then a gasp when I tightened it a little further.

"Breathe," I whispered.

She did as instructed, and after a moment, her look went soft, went almost hazy with lust. The pain had morphed into the sweet pleasure she loved.

"Brax," she whispered as I repeated the motions for her other nipple.

Only when they were both affixed and she'd felt their bite, then bliss, did I step back.

"Look at our mate, Captain. Beautiful without, and with."

She'd never worn the chain before, but the sight of it, with the dark green gems swaying beneath her pert nipples, made it one step closer to claiming her as mine, had my balls aching. The need to bend her over the bed and fuck her from behind as her breasts swayed, as the chain swung, was almost desperate.

I would take her that way. Soon.

Her gaze shifted to Trist and I saw the touch of uncertainty. Surely, he felt it through their collars.

He pushed off the wall, strode over to her. He looked down at her breasts, studied them silently. With one finger, he flicked the chain, set it in motion. She gasped.

"She likes it," he said, as if that had been a surprise for him.

I moved behind her, reached around and cupped a breast with one hand, and settled the other between her thighs. I had missed her slick heat, always wet, always dripping for me.

"Trist," she breathed.

"You like his touch."

"Yes."

"I felt how much you like the clamps. I admit, seeing my color upon you makes me wish to fuck you."

"Trist," she repeated.

He stepped back, but didn't tear his gaze away. I took it as my signal to continue. The hand that had only cupped her pussy began to play, to slide over her folds, slip fingers deep inside her, to pull out and circle her clit, again and again. She began to writhe, to ride my hand in her need to come. It set the chain in motion, which made the gems sway, which tugged on her nipples.

"Yes!" she said again, this time all doubts, all worries gone. She was lost to the pleasure I worked from her body.

I imagined the collar about her neck made Trist feel her need and in turn, she no doubt felt his. He might not say it, but he was turned on by the sight of Miranda being touched by another. She was able to give over her control to me because she sensed his satisfaction. He might not like me, personally, but he liked how I cherished her body.

"You are ready, *gara*," I said when she'd all but drenched my hand with her arousal.

She nodded against my shoulder, and I walked her forward toward the bed until she was standing directly at the foot of it.

"Bend over, *gara*. I will fuck you now. I will ease your pussy's need for my cock."

Eagerly, she set her hands on the bed, ass up. She gasped as her action set the chain in motion, her nipples taking the sweet brunt of it all.

Trist grabbed the chair and moved it a few feet from the bed, and settled in it, legs spread. Miranda was in profile to him and he would be able to see every inch of her as she got fucked.

I opened my pants and pulled out my cock. While remaining clothed wasn't as intimate, I wanted Trist to only see our mate. I wasn't bothered by him seeing me naked. I wasn't modest, not when it came to pleasing our female. But this was all about Miranda.

Gods, it would *always* be about pleasing her.

I slid a finger over her plump, pink folds, dripping and ready for my cock.

Stepping close, I took her then, slid deep in one long stroke until I bottomed out.

"Brax!" she screamed, her inner walls clenching about me.

"*Fark*," I growled, reveling in the hot, wet feel of her as she all but strangled my cock. It had been five weeks and I'd missed this. Missed her.

Gripping her hips, I took her, hard.

Out of the corner of my eye, I saw Trist open his pants, pull out his cock and stroke it.

"Yes!" Miranda shouted. Obviously his burst of pleasure hit her as well.

Her breasts swayed with each thrust, the chain in constant motion. Fuck, it looked so good on her. I awaited the day it was affixed to rings that were through her nipples and not clamps. In the meantime, she would know what it would feel like, I would know what it looked like, and Trist, he would discover his mate needed more. So much more than a rigid Prillon could ever offer.

"I'm coming," she moaned, just before I felt her walls ripple around me.

I couldn't hold back a second longer, the tight feel of her pulling the cum from my balls. I thrust deep, gripped hard and filled her.

When my brain began to function again, when I was no longer blind from the strength of my orgasm, I looked to Trist. His gaze was on Miranda, panting and gripping the bed as if it were the only thing keeping her from floating off into space.

I pulled out, took male satisfaction in watching my cum seep from her.

Miranda remained in place, but I hooked a hand about her waist again, helped her to stand.

I kissed the shell of her ear, then murmured, "Your mate, *gara*. He needs you."

I watched as her eyes fluttered open and she looked to Trist. Her hand went to her collar as if she could feel his need as much as see how hard his cock was, how pre-cum seeped from the small hole at the top.

"Go to him and give him what he needs."

She took a step toward him and I slapped her ass. Her head whipped about to eye me with confusion. I narrowed my gaze and crossed my arms. Waiting. Oh, I was sure I was not as stern as I could be with my slick cock, still hard and ready for her again, sticking out of my open pants.

"Yes, Master," she whispered, a small smile playing about her lips.

My cock was ready to go again, for those words from her lips were the closest thing to heaven on a battleship.

∾

Trist

. . .

FUCK, she liked it. No, she *loved* it. The collars made it obvious. So did the look on her face, the way her body went lax, the way she gave herself over to Brax so beautifully.

There was no question she submitted to me, but this was different. It was as if there was a second side to her that I didn't know, that responded to Brax in a way I could never elicit. This was what I'd expected from a second.

But from the Trion doctor? From the male who'd hurt my mate? I'd felt her sadness, although I hadn't known it was because of him until his arrival. Then I understood. She wanted him, but he'd refused.

His loss was definitely my gain, but had I gained all of her? It had been less than two days that she'd belonged to me. Oh, she was mine. I didn't doubt that or question it. But was she his, too?

He might know what made her hot, what made her come, some deep secrets and dark fantasies she didn't want fulfilled with me.

But that didn't make him a worthy mate. I questioned his ability to be my second, for a second was stalwart. He stood fast with his family. He put his mate first before work, before everything.

Would he do that? Could he do that?

I didn't know the answer. One fuck and nothing was solved. I learned so much about Miranda, what she needed, but nothing more.

Brax, whose seed slipped down her thighs as she approached, would need to earn more than just the title of Master. He would have to earn the word Second.

When Miranda stood before me, her legs between my parted knees, she paused. I continued to stroke my cock as I took in every inch of her. I was relaxed in my chair, enjoying the sight of Miranda being fucked. It was arousing to see her so well-satisfied and her pleasure that I felt through my collar only made me want to stroke harder and finish myself, spurting my seed in an arc onto the floor. But no, it was for her, for her pussy, so I gripped the base tightly, staved off my need and just looked.

Those gems on her nipples, the pretty pink tips and the shiny green, the combination was mouth watering. And the green... it did something to me.

The chain that gently swung was pure adornment, but it did make her lovely. Made her feel lovely, per the collar. It was a restraint of sorts and I wondered if she liked to be tied up, to be bound to a bed and at her mates' mercy.

"Trist," she whispered, and I met her eyes. "Please."

That was all she had to say. I was ready. I knew she was. Knew she was wet enough to take me. Hell, her thighs were covered.

Lifting my hand from my cock, I hooked my finger in the chain and used it to coax her to lean forward. I didn't tug, only used it as a guide, for she followed, knowing the bit of pain that would come if I were denied.

Her lips met mine in a fierce, swift kiss.

When I pulled back, I hooked a hand about her ass, pulled her so she straddled my lap, up on her knees.

"Ride me, mate."

She lowered herself quickly, but I held her fast.

"Slow," I commanded.

She huffed out a breath and settled upon my cock so her thighs rested on mine. I was so deep, so far within her I didn't know where she ended and I began.

Her hands settled on my shoulders and she began to move, to lift up.

"No," I said.

"Trist..."

"Who is in charge, mate?"

She swallowed and her dark eyes were on my mouth.

I leaned forward and kissed her, gave her what she wanted. At least part of it.

"You are," she whispered when I rested my head back against the tall chair back.

"But this... my cock inside you, is not enough."

Her eyes flared wide and I felt fear and guilt course through the collar.

"You are enough. Trist, I'm not trying to hurt you."

I wasn't hurt. But the understanding was a struggle.

"Brax's cock is still hard. He still wants you. Wherever shall he put his cock?" I asked.

She dripped all over me at those words, her inner walls clenching. Yes, I'd been right.

My hand on her hip slid to her ass, then my fingers dipped into the crack, found her snug back entrance.

I hadn't used the ATB with her. Yesterday, my cock had been enough. I'd planned to train her ass using the Prillon mating box meant for new brides, specifically those from other planets. But I somehow knew that wasn't necessary.

"She likes ass play," Brax said.

I looked over Miranda's bare shoulder to the Trion, who was tucking his cock back into his pants.

"Keep that out. She wants it."

I flicked my gaze to Miranda, saw the truth on her face.

"Here."

I pressed my thumb to her ass, circled, then slid it into her. Her ass accepted it easily and she gasped, wiggled on my lap.

I let her fuck herself on me, which only worked my thumb into her even deeper.

I widened my knees until she was opened too. Her feet

didn't touch the floor and she had no balance, giving her no choice but to hold on to my shoulders.

"You need two males in you at once, don't you, mate?" I asked.

She looked to me. Nodded. She couldn't lie. Not only because of the collars, but because of the match.

"You are a Prillon bride. You wouldn't have been matched to me otherwise."

I slipped my thumb free and she moaned.

"Lube, in the drawer beside the bed."

Brax went where I told him, found the vial and liberally coated his cock. Once done, he brought the vial with him and knelt behind Miranda. His cock was hard even after fucking her. I understood this, for mine hadn't gone down since she'd transported to the battleship.

"Ready, mate?"

She nodded and Brax reached about and cupped her breasts, holding her in place for his entry. I knew the second he pushed in, breached that tight hole. I felt him through the thin membrane that separated us. Felt it through the collars. Saw the intensity of it flare in her eyes.

"Trist," she groaned. Writhed, although there was nowhere for her to go.

I felt her pleasure, her heat. With my hands on her hips, I lifted her almost completely off my cock. I'd barely moved since she first settled upon me and I was desperate for the slide, the friction.

Brax slid out the same amount, then I lowered her down. Double fucked, double filled.

She let her head fall back as the two of us took her. The need built, swirled. Our breaths mingled, our skin slick with sweat. We felt complete, whole, with her between us. I was going to come, I couldn't hold back much longer, but she would find her pleasure again first.

And so I did the one thing I knew would set her off, the one thing I never expected to do. I reached up, opened both of her nipple clamps at the same time.

Her eyes flared as the blood rushed back to the tender tips. I felt the flood of pain, the flush of heat, the gush of wetness and heard her scream of pleasure.

It was too much, too great to resist and I followed her over. Brax stiffened and growled as his cock pulsed to fill her ass.

I sensed her contentment settled between me and Brax. He could give her pleasure, that was not in question.

But everything else? Time would tell. Until then, I'd let my sleeping mate rest, for I had plans for her.

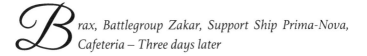

*rax, Battlegroup Zakar, Support Ship Prima-Nova,
Cafeteria – Three days later*

MIRANDA WAS LAUGHING with a group of four Prillon children, working together to make some kind of food, and not with the S-Gen machine. The youngest, a small female, was perhaps six years old. The eldest a boy of eleven or twelve. He had an ion blaster strapped to his thigh, which I kept my mouth shut about. I didn't know if it was armed or if it were a training pistol used to teach a child responsibility and proper care of such a weapon and to ensure he became accustomed to constantly wearing one.

On Trion, we did not arm children. This was a war zone though, and he was Prillon, as tall as Miranda already, even at his young age. He appeared to be enjoying the extra attention from the new Lady Treval as much as the rest of them. I didn't blame the boy, for I was enamored by her as well.

I had no idea how much honor, adoration and responsibility the mates of these warriors were blessed with upon their arrival in space. It was a dangerous place filled with constant tension, possible threat, imminent battles. Potential death. Commander Zakar himself had warned me from disrespecting any lady in the battlegroup at peril of my life. They not only gave of themselves to their mates—and for a Prillon match she had to contend with two alpha, bossy males—but to the people of the battlegroup as well. Big, small, young and old, they all wanted the ladies' attention.

Not that I needed the warning from Zakar. I was Trion, not an idiot. I did not disrespect females, but the social structure within a battlegroup was fascinating. The warriors were in charge of all things military, and their mates were equal to them in rank on the civilian side. In fact, when it came to domestic disputes or living arrangements, any part of day-to-day life, Lady Zakar out-ranked her mate, the commander of an entire battlegroup. As for the children, they adored the ladies, worshipped them like mythical creatures and craved their attention.

I'd read all of this, of course, back in my school days when we learned about the different planets and their unusual cultures, but seeing it in action was completely different. Watching Miranda blossom with such joy was sobering indeed. I could not have offered her this on Trion. It showed how incomplete a life she would have had there with me. That perhaps she'd been correct in walking away from me and being tested. The children with her were lucky, but so was I.

I would miss the sun, the sand and the fresh breeze on my face only found on Trion. If I could have Miranda, I would learn to live without. It would not be a hardship when I could see her smiling face. Hear her laugh, her moans of pleasure, feel the way her pussy clenched my cock, watched as she pleased her other mate. Even now, I hardened with want for her. Yet even with the knowledge I could sink into her sweet heat every night, space was more of an adjustment than I'd been anticipating.

Who the fuck was I kidding? I'd foolishly thought to arrive, steal her away from whatever idiot she'd been mated to, and transport back to Trion. I'd thought to take her from her new mate and give up nothing.

I sighed, ran a hand over my face. I'd been a fool. More than a fool. Selfish. Idiotic. Gods, I didn't deserve her. In that, Trist was right. I wasn't worthy to be her mate if I thought of myself first. I couldn't give her up though. I wouldn't. No matter the cost to my pride, my ego, or even my life, she would be mine. I would share her with a big Prillon warrior who was gruff and severe with everyone but Miranda. With her, he changed. He was... more. He knew that having a mate required sacrifice, accommodation. Transformation.

I did. Now. And that made me an idiot. But I was trying.

Miranda chose that moment to laugh as the young Prillon girl had done something to create a cloud of the strange white powder she called *flour,* something from Earth used to make sweet foods. The flour hovered in the air before settling on her head. She had lovely copper colored hair, and the white powder made her look very silly indeed. I couldn't help but smile.

The entire group laughed as Miranda hugged the mischievous young one. All of them were smudged with the flour, but no one seemed to mind. Her dark green gown was coated and smudged with the stuff, especially the curve of her breast beneath the clinging fabric. That green was Trist's color. Trist's claim. It seemed a cruel irony that the jewels in the adornments I had designed and used upon her were the same color. I imagined how my adornments would hang

from those round nipples pierced with rings, how the gold
medallions would hang between on a thin chain and tug on
her nipples to keep her constantly aroused. My cock grew
harder still watching her glow with happiness, with contentment and a sense of peace I'd never seen on her face before.

The flour was inconsequential. As were the rest of the
ingredients for the cookies I'd heard Roark talk about back
on Trion. Miranda had a love for something called *baking,*
making edible food by hand. I was perfectly content with
the S-Gen machine and had never seen flour, butter or eggs
before, but the experience of teaching the children how to
do this *baking* obviously made my mate... no, *Trist's mate,*
very happy.

I thought of the lucky warrior. Trist's smile was pure
adoration for his female and never in my life had I been so
envious of another male. The three of us had transported
together to this support ship. Trist had a meeting with the
crew and he hadn't wanted Miranda far from his side.

I was in complete agreement for once, not wanting to
leave her side either. I joined them. There was not a chance
I would let the two of them go off on their own. If I were to
win at least part of Miranda's heart, I needed to be with her,
not lazing about on the main battleship.

He, too, watched our mate. Yes, she *was* mine, gods be
damned. He'd returned from his meeting with the crew and
leaned against the wall near the door, arms crossed, a look
on his face I knew well. I'd felt that way when she'd been
mine. Or at least been in my bed back on Trion. I'd been
content. Full of desire and possessive urges and the need to
protect.

Even here on a support ship, I worried for her safety.
Trist did as well, and I didn't need a collar to sense that. It
seemed she, too, had an important purpose in visiting the

ship, something about meeting the crew on all the ships as she was the new second in command to Lady Zakar.

What a responsibility and yet she was enjoying it, making a mess and having fun. He went to his meeting, and I sat in this room, watching the female I cared about happily explore her new life and her new role as the important and influential Lady Treval. I stared at the black collar around her neck and knew it would be green before long. She still had nearly three weeks to decide if Trist was the mate for her, although I knew she didn't need that time. She was sure of the match. She was in love... and not with me. Not anymore. I'd totally fucked that up.

From the way she kept looking up at Trist, her heart in her eyes and desire flushing her skin, I realized, for the first time, the true enormity of my mistake.

Trist kept nothing from her. Not his need, his desire, his heart, his vow to protect and cherish her. Where I'd been a coward, he was bold in his feelings, claiming her for the entire universe to see and recognize. And the connection they shared through the collars, he couldn't hide a thing from her, even if he wanted to. I had no doubt that if anyone in the Fleet threatened her, Trist would tear that person limb from limb without a second thought. And she knew it, too.

Even I knew what she meant to him. Everything. Fucking everything. The stars and moons and reason for drawing breath.

If she and I had worn collars during our months of... of *friends with benefits,* perhaps things would have turned out differently. She'd have known how I felt, even when I hadn't. But I'd been a fool and kept my feelings from her when she was in my arms, my bed. I'd denied my truest intentions. I'd been selfish, excusing my lack of honesty with her by convincing myself I was doing it for *her,* when the truth was that I'd only been thinking about what was easier for myself. I didn't want to hold her again and walk away. I didn't want to see her cry. I didn't want to know that she was worrying about me, or missing me, or needing me when I wasn't there for her. I made the mission my priority and my weakness second.

But would she have been happy? Would she have been whole? The Brides Testing clearly showed she wanted more than I could give her. She wanted the dependability and structure of a Prillon. She wanted two mates. While Trist was definitely one, I wanted to be the other.

Miranda had been last on my stupid priority list and that's why I was here now, on a Prillon support ship trying to prove myself to one of the toughest, meanest bastards I'd ever met.

Oh, he wasn't that way with her. I'd seen exactly how much he bent for his female.

But ask anyone on the battleship, in the entire battle-group—and I had been doing just that for the last two days—and to a warrior I was informed that Trist was the coldest, most calculating, toughest, most honorable, battle-hardened warrior in the Fleet.

Which was just my fucking luck. I didn't have to win over a jovial or even accommodating male. No, Miranda had been matched to someone who was just as much a bastard as I.

If our roles were reversed and he'd been the one to break Miranda's heart, I probably would have killed him.

My only saving grace was the way Miranda looked at me, the way her emotions toward me, even ones I didn't understand, were felt by Trist. No doubt, his magical collars were the only reason I was still alive. Miranda still cared for me, despite all my failings. I knew her. Knew her body. Her heart. She was softness and light, so sweet and submissive. So trusting and pure of heart. She needed a hard bastard to protect her, to keep her safe—both mentally and physically.

For a while, the tough bastard had been me. And I'd failed.

I wasn't surprised at Trist's strength of character. His dominant nature. He was fucking perfect for her. And if I were being honest with myself—a new oath I'd made after my first night of sleeping alone—I admired him. He *was* good for her. He would never fail her, never betray her.

But after we'd taken her together, Trist hadn't allowed me to touch her again. We'd taken her many times that night, sometimes both of us touching her together, other times fucking her individually, the other watching. He'd told me I'd proven my ability to pleasure her, but not to protect her. I was Trion. Small. Weak. Even being part of the I.C. and a doctor, I had to prove myself to *him* now, not as Miranda's lover, but as a worthy second. Someone of honor. Someone who would keep her safe and happy, not just in the bedroom, but out of it.

And fuck me if that wasn't going to be a lot tougher than making Miranda whimper and beg for more in bed. He'd kicked me back to my own quarters since that one night. I slept alone while he held her at night. Wrapped her in his arms and made love to her.

While other Prillon males paraded around in front of her, bowed before her, kissed her hand and offered their protection in front of Trist. He hadn't taken any of them up on their offer. Yet.

But he could. Any moment, any one of them could steal her away from me forever.

Fark. Fark. Fark.

Maybe I could just challenge Trist to a duel.

Even as my blood began to boil at the thought of being denied, I caught Miranda meeting his gaze once again and sighed. She loved the bastard. I knew that look. Once upon a time, that look had been directed at me.

Again, I was being selfish. Fighting Trist would only hurt her. And the other, even more disturbing thought that had been running through my mind since our bed play? She'd been matched to Prillon Prime. She'd shattered into a million pieces sheltered between us that night. She *needed* two mates to be truly happy. Two mates for protection, security and loving. Which meant I either came to grips with the idea of sharing her, or I had to walk away.

And *that* was not fucking happening.

The kids made little round balls of their creations and placed them on tiny metal sheets. Lined up behind them on a table were four small devices Miranda called *toaster-ovens.* They carefully slid the sheets inside, careful not to burn themselves—the little machines were dangerous as could be —and Miranda instructed them to turn a circular knob on the front to set the time.

I didn't know what any of that meant, but she tried to explain to me that the box would heat the flour mixture, dry it out, and that would be when the white stuff she called *cookies,* would be ready to eat.

Why add the liquid in the first place when she needed the flour to be dry in order to eat it?

I didn't understand, but she was happy and no one burned themselves from the fire traps, so I sat and watched and made sure nothing threatened her. That was my job as a potential second, was it not? And sleeping alone, I had come to realize that I very much wanted to be with her, as a first, second or tenth, I didn't care. She was mine and I had every intention of correcting my mistakes and earning her trust again, even if that took the rest of my life.

The kids had just finished washing their hands when an alarm sounded.

Miranda froze and looked immediately to Trist, her mate, to keep her safe. "What is that?"

He looked at me across the room, and I moved closer to Miranda and the kids, placing myself between them and the door. I knew that sound. It was universal within the entire Coalition Fleet. That was a battle alarm. Why here and now was the question.

Trist took up position in front of the door and placed his hand on his comm. "This is Trist. Report."

Nothing but static answered him and he drew his ion blaster. I didn't have one, as Trist had pointed out—with great pleasure—that I was a doctor, not a warrior.

Well, fuck that.

I jogged to the S-Gen machine. "Ion blaster, gradient zero-one-zero."

"Authorization code?" The computer buzzed and Trist turned to me with shock in his eyes. I ignored him.

"This is Doctor Valck Brax, Intelligence Core, clearance level zero-one-zero, access code Earth Miranda Doyle."

"Voice confirmed. Code correct. Complete biometric scan."

"Brax, what are you doing?" Miranda was moving closer, wringing her hands before her as she glanced to the children. "And why did you say my name?"

"I'm protecting you." Apparently, all of my code clearances were still in the Coalition Fleet's system, and thank the gods for that. If this ship had communication blackout by Hive attack forces, I wouldn't have been able to access a weapon unless my information was already stored in their system.

I stepped onto the black scanner pad lined with bright green bars and waited. This part always burned a bit, as the scan was more intense than the normal used for clothing measurements. Not many knew the scanners were also capable of becoming transport pads, but Trist would know. As did I. And the weapon I'd requested was way above a doctor's grade, reserved for Intelligence Core operations or battleship commanders.

As for the access code *Earth Miranda Doyle,* it was the one I'd been using for the last two years since her arrival on Trion with Natalie and baby Noah. My obsession with her did not weaken or fade with time. I didn't want to talk about that. Not right now.

The S-Gen machine's bright green light faded. "Scan complete. Please clear transport pad."

I stepped back and waited as a special black weapon appeared. Not a typical ion blaster, this one could ionize an enemy completely. Not simply injure or burn, but turn an enemy into particles smaller than dust. They were top level clearance only. Even Trist didn't have one. They were not battle issue, as the I.C. did not want them falling into the hands of our enemy Hive.

I wrapped my fingers around the handle and grinned at Trist, raising my brows. "So, what's this alarm all about?"

"You lied to me, *Doctor,*" he said, his voice calm and accusatory, even with the alarm blaring.

I shook my head. "You banished me to private quarters and didn't bother to ask about my background."

His eyes narrowed. "We will discuss this later."

The young Prillon boy made his way to my side, and I

shifted my attention to him. "Do you know how to use that blaster?"

He looked offended, which had been my intention. Better angry than scared. "Of course. My fathers have taught me well."

"Good." I nodded and put my hand on his shoulder. "Take the rear and be ready in case they transport in behind Lady Treval or the other children."

"Who? In case *who* transports in?" Miranda asked as she watched the young warrior reassure his little sister before moving into position behind her and the other three much younger children. The Prillon boy pulled his blaster from where it had been strapped to his thigh—clearly not a practice weapon—and turned his back on us, watching the other side of the room. Good lad. Well-trained.

"The Hive, mate. Remember the other day when we were in the command deck and there was talk of ships disappearing? I fear this ship is their next target." Trist looked at me and I returned my attention to the door.

"Comms are dead?" I asked.

"Yes." His dark look said it all. We'd be fighting our way out of here.

13

WHAT THE HELL was going on? I'd never heard that sound before, but I instinctually knew it wasn't good. Not the way Brax and Trist were behaving. The way the children stopped what they were doing and lined up quietly. Orderly. It reminded me of a fire drill in elementary school on Earth. But we weren't walking outside. There was no outside.

The fire department wasn't coming. The Hive was.

Here? On this ship? On this silly little ship where I was baking *cookies?* Even now the scent of vanilla and cinnamon Snickerdoodles filled the air. Damn Hive. They were going to try to hurt us, and they were going to make me burn my cookies. Okay, I shouldn't be so flippant about the Hive, especially with children here.

"Trist?" I asked. "What do you want me to do?"

"Do not fear, Miranda." He looked over his shoulder at me where he stood in front of the door and I felt something

I'd never felt from him before. Fear. Not that he would die, but that something would happen to *me*. He probably wasn't too keen on me knowing his inner thoughts and feelings at this moment, but it definitely helped me remain calm, to judge just how much danger we were in. If he were to protect us, then I needed to keep my wits about me. I needed to stay calm for the children.

"I will allow nothing to harm you, mate," he vowed.

I sensed his resolve, his complete devotion to me. His willingness to die to keep me safe. To keep the children of others safe. That last bit truly scared the shit out of me. I didn't want him to die. I needed him to live. I hadn't even told him I loved him yet. I hadn't even accepted his claim, my collar still black. And black was *not* my color. I loved him. I did. I knew it that first night when I'd been with both him and Brax. I had become even more sure when he'd banished Brax to the visitor's quarters and spent the next two nights making love to me, pushing my boundaries, exploring the dark needs I'd not shared with him before Brax came into the picture. My nipples hardened at the memory.

Not the time! *Not* the time, nipples.

It turned out Trist loved dominating me, body and soul. He'd learned quickly that the bossier and more demanding he became, the more powerful my response. Now *that* had been a time when the collars came in handy. I still loved Brax, part of me always would, but I knew now that I would be happy with whatever Trist decided. Submitting to him, in bed and out, was what I wanted. Craved.

Needed.

And if he didn't feel Brax was worthy, I would accept that, accept a new warrior into my bed. Trist was mine and I was his. I loved Brax, but I would not sacrifice my new life, this new happiness, to have him. If Brax couldn't accept that, then he didn't really love me. It saddened me to think it, but one thing this Brides testing thing had taught me was that I didn't have to compromise. I could have it all. I deserved it.

I would not accept less than total devotion from a mate. Even a second. I deserved better. Trist had reinforced those thoughts.

Trist blocked the door with his body so I couldn't see beyond him.

Then Brax blocked my view of Trist.

The young man who'd been happy to smile, laugh, make cookies and tease his little sister was now standing at our backs with an ion blaster drawn in a battle stance. I'd thought it humorous he'd worn the pistol in a holster, just like a gunslinger in the Wild Wild West, or a kid with a pop gun playing grown up. He wasn't *playing* at anything, I realized. His sister had flour in her hair, but she obviously loved and trusted her older brother, and he was prepared to protect her, just as Trist was for me. When he'd touched her on the head as he walked past, she'd smiled and relaxed her hold on my hand.

The young man whispered to her, softly, but I heard him.

"Don't worry. I will protect you." Yes, just as I thought. Prillons raised their boys well.

Her smile was one-hundred percent love and complete trust. "I know."

She stood next to me, stoic and unafraid, as the other two younger children clung to my side as if their world was about to end.

And Brax? He'd worked the S-Gen machine like a pro and had created a black space gun that looked even nastier than the one Trist had pointed at the closed door. Seemed there were things we didn't know about Brax after all.

"Try comms again," Brax said.

"I did. No one is coming," Trist replied, jaw clenched.

Brax tensed, his back going rigid. "The S-Gen is too small to transport us out of here."

I looked to the machine like the one I'd used to make ice cream on Trion. It transported people? God, I could have sent myself to Rogue 5 by mistake!

"We have no comms," Trist replied. "We can't reach the Zakar and we can't initiate transport from here."

Brax took a moment to digest that and I did, too. My men thought the ship was under attack and we had no way to contact the battleship... or anyone else. Or transport from this spot. Leaving this room... "What are your orders?"

Trist leaned around Brax to glance at first me, then the children. "We make a run for the shuttle. Can you fly?"

Brax nodded. "Yes."

"Rating?"

While Brax rattled off a list of stuff that made no sense to me, but satisfied Trist—and surprised him, a reaction I felt via the collars—I had to keep myself busy. If I just stood about feeling useless, I'd go crazy. So, I cleaned, which was ridiculous since we were leaving the room any minute. But the kids saw I was calm, that things weren't so bad that I felt it okay to organize the supplies. I even wiped off the counter as best I could with my hands. What a mess.

Baking was messy.

A sound filled the air and moments later the door slid open.

Trist stepped back, weapon raised...

Nothing. The corridor beyond was empty.

With a curse, Trist fired his blaster into the seemingly empty space.

I winced and wanted to cover my ears, but I dashed to the girls and wrapped my arms about them.

A heavy thump followed and Trist fired again and again, at nothing.

Something rolled toward Trist on the floor.

"Get down!" Trist screamed and threw his chest over the thing.

I doubled over, my ears ringing as a shrill whistle filled the room, followed by a blinding flash.

"Plasma bomb!" Brax cursed and moved into position at Trist's side, firing at the same nothing as my mate attempted to lift himself off the floor.

What were they firing at? Where had the plasma bomb come from?

Brax fired again, using one hand placed beneath Trist's arm to help him up. On the floor, just outside the door, a dead body appeared as if out of thin air. It was like magic, one second invisible, the next... there. The creature had a Prillon's face, except it was half dark copper skin and half a bright, shiny metal that looked like polished chrome. His body was covered by a strange, shimmering armor that I'd never seen before, but it almost looked like glitter. Holographic glitter.

Why was a Prillon firing at us? What was all over him?

I tugged the children and we ducked down behind the table where we'd been baking as Trist bellowed in pain. I winced, then panicked when I smelled burning flesh. His agony blasted me through the collar so that I fell to my knees and gasped with the intensity of it.

"Trist!" I screamed, but Brax bellowed at me before Trist could respond.

"Stay down!"

I tucked the girls' heads down, but knew Trist had been hurt. No enough to stop him, but he was hurting. Definitely injured by that plasma bomb.

Beside us, the young Prillon, Var, began firing his weapon as well. He shouted a warning. "More back here!"

"Go!" Trist yelled at Brax and the man I'd only ever seen as a lover, or a doctor, leaped across the room to assist the young Prillon with the speed of an Everian Hunter I'd met once on Trion. Brax shot and fired his special gun and one enemy magically appeared dead on the floor. I understood now this was the Hive. This was the enemy I'd heard about but never believed existed when I'd been on Earth. Why were they invisible? Brax didn't let up, exchanging ion blasts with more attackers. It was odd to see him firing at someone he couldn't see. Not until they were dead and then they appeared, it seemed.

The little girl watched her brother, still unafraid. She caught me looking, and the faith I saw in her eyes nearly broke my heart all over again. "Var won't let them hurt me. He's strong, like our fathers."

How did someone so small seem so confident, so assured at a time like this? I was the one to be the example, but it seemed she was an example to me. I ran my hand through her hair. "Yes, he is."

Two more blasts aimed at Brax. It appeared the invisible intruders believed him to be more of a threat than the young Prillon. They were right.

But he couldn't *see them* to fire back.

I stared at the flour coating the young girl's hair and a thought came to me like a plasma bomb explosion.

"Yes!" Elation filled me as I was struck by an ingenious

idea. Apparently, Trist felt my excitement, and my determination to help.

"Stay down!" Trist commanded.

Too late. I was on my feet, the bowl filled with unused flour in my hand. Desperate to help, I ran around the edge of the table, throwing flour into the air as I went. First to Brax and Var. Three handfuls of flour caught the air like pixie dust in a Disney movie and the unseen became ghosts coated in white.

"Brilliant, mate!" Brax yelled as he and Var took down the intruders with much more accurate shots.

I turned to see if Trist needed any help finding his invisible opponents, but he had two dead bodies at his feet. The third intruder I could not see, but he grappled with Trist in a physical struggle. It was the strangest thing, as if Trist were possessed, shifting and kicking, punching and firing at... nothing.

Screw that.

I ran as close as I dared and threw more flour into the air where I knew, logically, Trist's assailant had to be. One handful. Two.

The invisible enemy turned white. He was huge, and not Prillon.

Brax saw the enemy as well. His eyes widened. "A fucking integrated Atlan. Gods help us."

He fired at Trist's attacker, shoving me behind him now that he could see the enemy. Over and over the blaster fire struck the huge Hive warrior. Terrified Brax would shoot Trist accidentally, I couldn't tear my gaze from the fight for survival raging before me.

"Take him out!" Trist ordered. Using a strength I could only imagine, he lifted the Hive off his feet and threw him several feet away.

The moment they were separated, both Brax and Var fired without stopping.

When the beast was down, unmoving, they stopped, both Brax and Var looking to Trist, who staggered back against the wall, his breathing ragged, his shoulders drooped with exhaustion.

Trist stared at the huge Atlan, bleeding and broken on the ground. I'd never seen anything so tragic in my life and tears gathered as I wondered about the giant who fought to get up. To keep fighting.

"There are nine of us." The Atlan pulled himself to a sitting position and turned his face to Brax. "Do it. End this torment."

Oh god. I remembered now. I'd heard about what the Hive did to those Coalition fighters they captured. They integrated them, some more than others, converting them into fighting machines so they attacked those who they used to serve with. It seemed this Atlan had not been fully integrated. He knew he was the enemy, that he was beyond saving. Beyond redemption. Death was the only release from the prison where the integrations in his body had him trapped.

He didn't want to fight us. He knew he was one of us, but could never be more.

God, it was so awful. I blinked back tears as Brax kept his blaster trained on the Atlan. adjusting something on the top of it. Brax addressed the warrior, the only Hive fighter still alive in the room. "Die with honor, brother."

The Atlan bowed his head and closed his eyes in obvious relief. "Thank you."

Brax bowed slightly at the waist and fired. The Atlan flashed so brightly I had to avert my eyes. When I turned back to look, there was gray dust, finer than flour, where the

Atlan had been moments before. I swallowed a lump in my throat, smiled down at the girls.

"Three more." Trist spoke into the quiet, his powerful frame sliding down the wall until he landed on his ass with a hard thump. His agony hit me as if he'd been holding it back, protecting me, and no longer could. As if he were losing consciousness.

"Trist." I rushed to his side, everything else forgotten. "Trist. Oh my god. You're hurt." And he was. His chest and shoulders were an oozing mess, as if he'd been on fire. Blood slowly pumped from his leg in a constant stream. I wasn't a doctor, but I knew that meant he had a severed vein, maybe even an artery. I'd taken basic first aid, but didn't spurting mean artery? No spurting. But still, god, he was dying.

Brax was at my side, pushing Trist onto his back. He turned to Var. "Watch the door. Count to three and fire. Keep that corridor clear."

"Yes, sir." Var moved into place and I was shocked to see his sister race to his side, bowl of flour in hand. She hid behind the door's frame, blindly throwing handfuls into the air in the corridor to help her brother.

So fierce, for children.

Brax gently moved me to the side and pulled his green doctor's tunic off over his head. Using it as a tourniquet, he yanked and pulled the fabric around Trist's thigh above the wound until Trist moaned in protest, but at least the bleeding slowed to a small trickle. "Miranda is going to be upset if you die, so get yourself together, Captain."

Brax's voice held the command that usually came from Trist.

Trist actually chuckled at that, but I was too stressed to appreciate that fact. I knew we had to get to a shuttle to save

Trist's life. And per the Atlan who'd given us the info and then asked to be put out of his misery, we knew there were three more of those... *things*... in our way.

I grabbed Trist's blaster thing out of his limp hand and pointed it at a chair. "Brax, show me how to use this thing."

"No." Trist started to protest, but I ignored him. "Now, Brax, or I'll never forgive either one of you."

When Brax hesitated, looking to Trist for permission, Trist lifted his hands to wrap around mine. Shaking and weak, he curved his fingers gently until I held the weapon in the proper position. "Aim, mate, and when you are ready, squeeze here."

It wasn't exactly like a trigger on a handgun back on Earth, but it was close. I took aim and blasted the stupid chair off its legs. Good. If any of those things thought they were taking one of my mates from me, they had another thing coming. And they better think twice about fucking with any children.

I turned to Brax, fierce and ready to end this. "Let's go. We need to get Trist out of here."

"Agreed." Brax looked grim, but not scared, and that gave me hope that we would all survive this mess. I knew he was more than just a doctor, but I hadn't talked about that with Trist during our time alone. I'd been much more interested in exploring... *other* things than talk about Brax and his secret missions—missions which I technically knew nothing about.

Missions that I was now grateful for, because he knew how to use a gun—some big-ass weapon like a Howitzer— and he could also fly us off this ship. Apparently, he could fly just about everything in the entire Coalition Fleet.

Brax was just one surprise after another.

But one problem remained. Trist was mine, and I would never leave him. "Can you carry him?"

Trist protested, but both Brax and I ignored him this time. "Of course," Brax answered. I sighed in relief.

"Good. Let's get the hell out of here."

I helped the remaining three children load up with small bowls full of flour as Brax hoisted Trist to his shoulders in a modified version of what I called a Fireman's Carry.

Trist was fading in and out, calling my name. I kept myself calm and focused on how much I loved him, how happy he made me. Good thoughts. Only good thoughts. It was my turn to protect him, even if it were to keep him calm through our collar connection.

"Let's go." Brax turned to Var. "I'll lead. Lady Treval behind me. Then the children. You guard our backs."

"Yes, sir." Var didn't even try to argue. That little warrior deserved some kind of freaking medal for this. And as Lady Treval, assuming we survived, I'd talk to Commander Zakar myself if I had to, and make sure he got one. The girls, too.

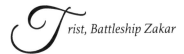
rist, Battleship Zakar

I NEVER IMAGINED BEING slung over the shoulder of a Trion trying to save my ass in battle. I hurt everywhere, but at the same time, not one specific spot was more painful than another. The haste with which Brax moved to get me to the med unit jostled my destroyed body, knocked the air from my lungs. The pain wasn't as bad as when I was first hit with the plasma bomb, but only because my skin had been burned off and no doubt the nerves were dead. Black dots filled my vision of the floor as well as Brax's ass, both of which made me want to pass out. I felt blood trickle down my leg, warm against the chill of my skin. I was dying. I was a warrior. I was prepared for my demise.

But not now. Not today. Things weren't set in place. As primary mate, I hadn't seen to Miranda's protection. To give her the second she deserved. She required.

I would die and she would be alone.

I was the worst of mates because she was not protected. She would not be cherished. Instead, lost and alone. Every male would be a threat. *Everything* would be a threat. There would be a challenge for the right to claim her. Another Prillon would take what was mine...

I heard voices, shouts. Commands. I saw feet and legs moving quickly, even from my upside-down position. I noticed the color of the walls, thought how they matched my family's colors. I loved green.

"I need a ReGen pod. Now!" It was Brax's voice, but with a snap of command to it that made him sound almost Prillon.

"Hurry, please. He's been badly injured." I recognized that soft voice, the one that lit up my life as bright as that fucking plasma bomb. Miranda. My mate. Even through my blurry haze of consciousness, I could feel her fear, her desperation. I wanted to ease her mind, but I couldn't, not because I couldn't move, but because I had not found a fucking second.

I was nudged off of Brax's shoulder and laid onto something soft. I groaned at the shift of muscle, the grind of bone on bone.

"Bleeding from the peroneal artery," Brax stated. "Tourniquet applied. Burns to forty percent of his body, specifically anterior chest and abdomen. Maximum pod time required."

"We should remove his clothes," someone said.

"Negative. The burns have bits of fabric in them. Removing them will only make things worse. He'll heal with his uniform on." Brax's voice was one of command and brooked no argument. I'd never heard that tone from him before. He sounded like... a commander. A warrior.

I opened my eyes. Blinked until things came into focus. I

lifted my arm to Brax, who was scanning my body with his eyes as if they were a wand and could heal me.

An actual wand, in someone else's hand, passed over my face. I felt no improvement, therefore, it must be only an injury scanner. I saw the curved lid of the ReGen pod move to enclose me, and I lifted my hand to stay its course.

"Wait," I said, my voice almost a whisper. I repeated it, using almost all my energy to make it loud enough to be heard over the calm chatter.

Brax whipped his head around to stare down at me.

"The pod is going to close. You will heal."

I shook my head, then winced. "Not yet."

He leaned down, gave me his penetrating dark gaze. The look of not only a doctor, but of a warrior in his own right. "Yes, now, or you will die and Miranda will be upset. That is not acceptable, Prillon."

If I could have chuckled, I would have. Here we were, back to arguing as we had upon his arrival.

"Here." I reached up with my other hand and tugged at the black collar wrapped about my wrist. I'd put it there to keep with me until I found a worthy second. Only then would I remove it. I hadn't thought it would be Brax. Hadn't expected him to be worthy of the honor.

But he was. He'd proven himself during the attack. Protected our mate. Saved my life, carried me from the battle and taken down the remaining Hive soldiers as we made our way to the shuttle that brought us back to the Zakar. He'd protected me, our mate, and the children who had been entrusted to our care. He was a worthy male.

It was I who was weak. Dying. It was I who'd avoided providing for the safety of a second for my mate because of my assumptions about Brax.

He was a good doctor. A good warrior. He would be a

good mate. Better than me since I'd failed Miranda in the most important thing of all—seeing to her happiness without me.

"Stop moving," Brax snapped. "You can be a bossy ass after you are healed."

"No. Now." My breathing was ragged as if I'd been fighting the Hive, not lying about. "This collar. It is for you, my second."

His eyes flared wide.

"Where is Miranda?" I breathed.

At those words, her head appeared above me alongside Brax. Ah, she was so beautiful, even with a smudge of smoke or dirt on her cheek, her hair long and tangled. She smiled at me, but it didn't reach her eyes as it usually did. I felt her anguish.

"Do not fear, Miranda," Brax said, as if he was wearing the collar now, as if he could sense exactly what she was thinking and feeling. "He will be fine if he'd let me lower the lid and let the pod do its work."

I ignored him and kept my eyes on hers. "I'm sorry, mate."

She gave me a watery smile. She leaned down close, so close I could smell her. Bright and like the flowers back on Prillon Prime. "There is nothing to be sorry about," she murmured. "You must heal now."

I tried to shake my head, but it hurt too much. "Not yet. Brax is your second. I will not allow healing until he is collared. Until I know you are protected."

Her mouth fell open, her eyes widened like the outer rings of this sector's third planet. "You want—"

"He is worthy," I growled, cutting her off. "He is honorable. If something happens to me—"

"Something already has," Brax reminded, glanced away

briefly as someone showed him a scan readout. He nodded, then looked back at me. "It is time."

"Yes, it is. Put the collar on. You are Miranda's mate as much as me. I will not allow the ReGen to begin until I know she is safe with you."

Brax stood to his full height, looked to Miranda. He kissed her forehead, then silently—and carefully—took the collar from my wrist.

Raising it to his neck, he closed it in place. All at once, I felt him as well. His emotions, his drive to save me. His protectiveness of not only Miranda, but me as well.

Miranda gasped, for his added sensations was intense.

Brax nodded once, gravely. "You have my word; I will protect our mate with my life."

I sensed his truth and I was satisfied. I sighed, gave over to the tug of unconsciousness, to the extent of my wounds. "Good."

"Heal, mate, or I will kill you myself," Miranda said, leaning down and gently cupping my cheek. Her words were full of threat, but her smile softened their meaning.

"With Brax around, we shall all remain safe," I replied.

Her fingertips slid gently over my cheek, then she stepped back and the lid was lowered. I looked at the two of them through the clear glass, my family, and felt their connection until the world went black.

rist, Private Quarters, Two days later

I FELT them before I saw them. My family. And gods help me, that now included the Trion doctor, Brax. He was not what I expected, the Trion male. More warrior than healer. Fiercely and completely in love with my mate before I knew of her existence.

But I felt their bond, even now, their emotions coming through my collar in a soothing familiarity that I knew my mate needed with me injured. Her pain and terror had been breaking me more than the agony of the plasma burns that covered nearly half of my body. And yet, once I'd accepted Brax, added his mental strength to our family bond, she'd calmed. His iron will and mental walls had wrapped around her and she'd calmed.

Even now, as I paused on the threshold of my own quarters, I could *feel* them both. His complete attention was on caring for her and making sure she was safe. Calm. And my mate? My female? The greatest gift the gods had ever blessed me with?

She was worried, the emotion an underlying simmer. But she was content. Not panicking. She felt... *safe.*

Brax was, indeed, a worthy second. Not only had he saved my life during the Hive attack, but he watched over our mate now, while I was unable, and made sure she was cared for. Loved. Protected.

I had chosen well. And despite the fact that Brax's foolish choices had driven Miranda from his arms, I could not help but be grateful for the strange twist of fate that had led them both to me.

The door to my private quarters slid open silently and I stepped inside to find Brax sitting on the sofa with Miranda curled up in his lap, asleep. Her face was pressed to his neck and she clung to him, even in sleep. She wore a soft gown in a style I'd never seen before, and assumed was from Trion. It was lovely, every shimmering inch of the material clung to her curves. She looked more dream than reality and my cock grew hard. I didn't want to wait to claim her officially. Make her mine. I didn't want any uncertainty, and now that I had decided upon Brax as a second, I only needed Miranda's consent to claim her forever. I had no doubts. I knew Brax—who had already followed her halfway across the galaxy—had none as well.

He lifted his head and indicated that I should be quiet. "She's only been asleep a few hours. She was worried about you," he whispered.

"I know. I could feel her." And I could, even while unconscious in the ReGen pod, I had dreamed of her and known she was near.

Making my way to the cleansing room, I removed the

medical garments they'd placed me in when I woke and stepped into the shower tube. The uniform I'd worn had been removed and disposed of and I did not miss the smell of burned flesh. Of battle.

Of Miranda's fear.

I did not linger, but washed away the last of the attack even as I wondered if Miranda would want both my collar and Trion adornments. The memory of her wearing the green gems had me wrapping my hand around my hard cock with a groan. Gods, she was beautiful. I didn't care what she wore. In fact, I preferred her naked. But it would be her choice, and I would honor Brax's traditions if that was what my female desired.

Anything for her. Anything to make sure she knew exactly how much I loved her. Needed her. I'd never needed another living creature. Not man nor beast. But now, I needed her. Not simply her presence, her joy in life. Her light. Her laughter and happiness. I needed to feel the contentment making her warm and sleepy and satisfied.

I was weary of this war, of killing. Of watching my friends and fellow warriors die. I needed a reason to keep fighting. And that reason was curled up in my second's lap, trusting him to protect her while I healed. Trusting me to return to her.

That trust was humbling, and I would not take it for granted.

I turned off the cleansing jets and dried quickly, returning to the main room where Brax and Miranda remained exactly as I had left them. I stood naked, eager to feel her in both body and mind.

But I was hungry now. Not for food, for her. It was time to claim her.

Brax looked me over and the grin on his face nearly made me chuckle. "Eager, are we?"

"And you are not?" I asked. "You are my second, Brax. If you accept the honor, and vow to protect both Miranda and any children we may have with your life."

His look turned from amused to serious. "Are you sure? I will not allow you to change your mind, Trist, simply because you were half dead when you gave me this collar. She's mine. Any child, yours or mine, I will love and protect. They will be part of her and I will fight to the death to keep her."

"I'm counting on it."

Our gazes locked and the bond we shared through the collars amplified what we were both feeling. Possessive. Protective. Aroused.

Miranda must have sensed something was going on, for she stirred. Her eyes opened and she looked up at Brax before she realized I was in the room. "Hi." Her smile was soft and accepting, full of trust. She loved him, the force of her emotion a shock to my system now that I could also feel Brax's love for her.

"Greetings, mate. Are you rested?" he asked, stroking a piece of hair away from her face with gentle hands.

"How is Trist?"

Brax burst out laughing and looked up at me. There was no resentment in his gaze, for he could feel her love as well as her worry for me.

Miranda turned her head, took one look at my naked body and cried out, scrambling from Brax's lap to leap into my arms. Her love for me hit me hard as I caught her. It was not the same as what she felt for Brax. For Brax, I felt her trust and desire, the feeling that she was pampered. He made her feel beautiful and desired.

Her feelings for me were a tangle of need and as she held me with all the strength in her small, human arms, squeezing as tightly as she could, clinging to me as if she could not breathe without me, I was content.

"Do you accept my claim, mate? Do you accept me as your primary male or do you wish to choose another."

"Shut-up, Trist. You're mine." She was crying and laughing at the same time, a skill I did not comprehend.

"Then you accept my claim?" Normally, this would be done in a room of Prillon warriors, chosen to honor the female and vow to protect her should anything happen to her mates, to come when called upon by her mates. But Brax was Trion, and I knew from the possessive way he watched us both now that he would not desire to share her in the traditional Prillon custom.

"Yes, Trist. I accept your claim."

Brax rose to his feet behind her and I noticed that he wore loose fitting clothing, which he quickly removed. When he was naked as well, he walked to one wall and opened a small storage compartment. He turned to me and Miranda, most likely sensing the sudden seriousness of his mood, released her hold enough to turn in my arms and face him.

"I had something made, Trist, back on Trion. I had it transported to the ship while you were healing." Brax walked forward and laid down a dark green fabric that was layered upon itself several times.

He unwrapped the contents and I saw not clamps, but piercing rings. They were on display in the shape they would take on our mate's body, one for each breast and one for her clit. There was a delicate gold chain hanging from the dark green gems attached to each ring, and within the links of that chain were small disks with alternating symbols. One was the symbol of House Treval, my house. The other I had never seen before, but I assumed the emblem belonged to Brax's family on Trion. There were also golden bangles for her wrists, decorated with green gems, and an elaborate necklace that looked like the delicate spinnings of a spider's web in gold and green. Two large rings were affixed at the top.

Brax looked pleased with himself. "I had them exchange half of the seals with the symbol for the Treval family of Prillon Prime."

They were beautiful and looked to be of the highest quality. Hand made, not produced from an S-Gen machine. The links were too delicate and imperfect.

Miranda slipped from my arms and dropped to her knees to inspect the gift, but she did not touch them. Instead, she looked to me for permission. Approval. I could feel her desire for them, but her need to please me came first. If I said no, she would put them away with no regrets.

That knowledge was humbling. "They are beautiful, mate. And they will look even more so upon your body."

Her smile brought me to my knees, and I slid down next to her and lifted the necklace from the soft fabric. "Lift your hair, Miranda. Let us adorn you."

Brax knelt on her opposite side and his anticipation fed mine. I could not wait to see our mate adorned in gold and green. The green matched the Treval family collars and would make our mate look like something out legend. A goddess made flesh.

With a grin I was beginning to enjoy too much, Brax slid one ring onto his finger and handed the other to me.

"What does this do?" I asked.

Miranda shivered, her lust a sudden inferno through the collars.

Interesting.

I looked at Brax and raised my brows.

He laughed. "You'll see."

rax

THIS WAS my dream come to life, not exactly the way I'd imagined, but better. Miranda needed Trist. I had wounded her, left her alone when she needed me those long months on Trion. I had broken a bond of trust—no, not broken, her previous male on Earth had done that—but I had reinforced the idea that she could not depend on a male to be there for her. To put her first. To make her a priority in his life.

Trist had healed that wound in her. Even now, as she lay sprawled out on the bed before me and I placed the piercings in her body, she looked to him for reassurance. Strength.

He kissed her, nuzzled her, pleasured her with his hand and mouth as I adorned our mate with the most beautiful emeralds I had been able to acquire. Each piercing healed instantly with the ReGen wand I held over her body. She felt no pain as I placed the green jewels on her luscious curves.

That the Treval family's mating collars were nearly the same color as the stones seemed a confirmation from the gods that everything had worked out exactly as it should.

Miranda was mine. I didn't have to give up my need to feel as if I were making a difference. Out here, doctors were in high demand, the stream of wounded warriors who needed life-saving attention nearly constant. The official transfer had been easy, once Commander Zakar saw the green collar around my neck. He'd clapped me on the back and welcomed me to the crew of Battleship Zakar.

I was part of this war now. Out here, in space. A turn I'd never expected my life to take. But then, I hadn't expected Miranda, either.

My mate's breasts were adorned beautifully and I placed my fingertips along the lips of her wet core to find her clit, teasing it from its hiding place to adorn it as well. Trist slid two fingers into her wet, eager pussy, her nipple in his mouth, his fingers slowly fucking her as I played with her clit, making her squirm before I placed the second ring.

She gasped, her hands twisted in the bedding even as her body arched beneath me. She was so aroused, so on fire for us both that my hands were shaking as I finished the second piercing.

That done, and healed by the ReGen wand, I set the wand aside and gave Trist the bracelets I'd ordered for Miranda's wrists. I knew she would not be wearing traditional Trion gowns here, on a Prillon battleship, and I wanted to be able to see her adornments no matter what she wore. The delicate circular bands were only the beginning. I had also purchased golden and emerald nets for her hair, rings for her toes and fingers, golden chains for her ankles and hanging gems for her ears.

With an intensity I, too, felt, Trist lifted first her left

hand, then her right, sliding a number of bracelets over each hand. We both stepped back, admiring our mate as she displayed herself on the bed, naked, adorned, beautiful beyond measure.

Aroused. Wet. Her pussy gleamed in the light nearly as brightly as the gold and jewels.

Now. I wanted her *now*.

I had no idea if the thought came from Trist or myself, but I wasted no time, walking straight to the drawer where the amazing lube device was kept. By the time I returned, Trist had moved in closer, his fingers trailing the links between her nipples and her clit as if hypnotized. He held out his hand and she looked like a queen as she placed her hand in his, her rings and bracelets flashing in the light in perfect complement to the chained jewels adorning her body.

"Gods, you are beautiful, Miranda." There was wonder in his tone. Awe. I felt the same.

His words pleased her, her happiness at his honest adoration a sensation like melted sweets coating my ragged heart. These collars were a gift from the gods themselves, and so was our female.

I added my devotion and desire to his, hitting her full blast as she strolled around our living quarters in her new adornments, the tension building. I was content to allow the moment to ride, build her anticipation, her pleasure. I was inclined to be patient.

Not so, her primary mate.

"Enough." Trist moved like the warrior he was, with speed, and she was gasping and laughing as he pressed her back to a wall and claimed her mouth.

"Do you accept my claim, Miranda? Or do you wish to choose another primary male."

There was no laughter in her voice when she answered him. "I already answered that question, Captain Treval. Do you have a hearing problem? Maybe I should choose a mate who can listen the first—"

Shock. Lust. Her back to the door. Trist had lifted her mid-sentence and impaled her on his cock, was pounding into her in a rhythm that had her head thrashing side to side as her breathe burst from her with each thrust of his hips.

"Maybe. You. Did. Listen."

He growled in response, his lips dropping to her fore-head as he fucked her. Hard.

"Damn it, Trist. Wait for me."

He turned his head and the feral smile I saw there let me know there would be no waiting, I would have to take what was mine, and I wanted to fuck her tight ass. Make her lose control. I wanted her to scream *my* name, not his. Mine.

I smiled back at Trist as Miranda's soft moans pushed me into action, the lube device in my hand.

Challenge accepted.

Miranda

THE WALL WAS hot against my back. Not cold. Not anymore. Trist's huge cock filled me and each thrust lifted me higher on the wall, his body hitting the new piercing in my clit, jostling the connecting chain that hung from my nipples. It was erotic. Sinful.

Fucking hot. God. So damn hot with Brax watching, waiting to pounce.

Lifting my arms above my head, I knew Trist would

respond immediately this time. He knew me now, knew what I needed.

I wasn't disappointed, his hand appeared to lock my wrists above my head, his grip tight but not painful, just hard enough to let me know I wasn't going anywhere until he was through with me. I was at his mercy, and my body lit up like fireworks as he fucked me. Hard. Harder.

Brax was watching. Waiting. He was like an Adonis, a dark and sensual god admiring his work. And I knew exactly what he was holding, the anal toy these Prillons had invented for their mates. Soon, he would be fucking me, too, his darker skin in contrast to my pale body and Trist's golden tones. His dark hair like silk in my fingers. His scent mixing with Trist's until I was drowning in them both.

Trist pounded into me and I tightened my legs around his waist, dug my heels into his hips. More. I wanted more. I wanted both of them.

He kissed my forehead, looked at Brax, then leaned down and nipped me on the ear. The shoulder. The smallest bite of pain, but it made me groan his name.

"Trist."

"Come for me, mate. Now. I want Brax to know who is pleasing you."

Brax? What would Brax think?

The blast of heat from both males hit me through our collars, and I lost control as Trist pushed deep, my pussy going into spasms all over his cock.

I shuddered, my body exploding as Trist held me trapped. I had no choice but to submit, surrender. And that pushed me higher, as aftershocks rolled through me, pushing me toward a second orgasm.

"Not yet, mate." That was Brax, his voice a growl next to my ear. I turned to the side to see him standing next to us.

"Brax."

He kept his eyes on me but spoke to Trist. "Turn around, Trist."

Trist released my wrists, his hands going to my ass as he did what Brax had asked. And it had been a request, of sorts. When it came to fucking me, it seemed a steady truce and understanding had been reached by my mates.

My mates. Mine. God. Both of them were mine.

Trist, his back to the door, lifted me by my ass, presenting me to Brax. Moments later, Brax's lips pressed to my shoulder as his fingertips found the tight opening of my ass and slipped the Prillon lube inside. Filled me with the warm fluid. Fucked me gently with the small toy before pulling it out.

My pussy rippled, clamping down on Trist like a fist and his groan seemed to drive Brax to hurry. He placed his cock at my opening and began to slide inside, stretching me, filling me until I was full, impossibly full of my two men, pressed between them, protected and safe and loved.

I shuddered and leaned my head back against Brax's chest, the only way I could touch him, let him know how much I loved him. Loved them both.

Love filled me up from somewhere deep inside, not an explosion, not orgasmic, but like the wind or the sunlight on my skin. Like breathing. It simply *was.*

Trist shuddered, his hands turning to vices on my hips. "Miranda."

Buried balls deep behind me, Brax held his hips still, his hands wrapping around me to play with the adornments on my nipples, trace the line of gold down my belly as he lowered his head and kissed me on the shoulder again. "Gods, female, you are going to kill us with that."

I laughed, I couldn't help it. "With what?"

"Love, mate." Trist's golden face was so solemn, so painfully beautiful. My mate, the one who made me feel completely safe, utterly perfect. The mate who had finally healed all the cracks and breaks in my heart. "With love."

They took me slowly, Trist with his gaze locked on mine as they fucked me, as if afraid I would disappear. Brax caressed every inch of my skin, played with the adornments the way I'd always imagined, making me feel beautiful. Claimed. Cherished.

We came together, my orgasm triggering both of them over the edge with me, and when it was done, both of my mates took great joy in inspecting my neck and the green collar that now made us a family.

EPILOGUE

Miranda, Natalie and Roark's quarters, Xalia City, Trion

THREE MONTHS later

"HOLY SHIT, MIRANDA. HE'S BIG." Natalie leaned in and whispered. "Is he big... *everywhere?*"

I couldn't help but laugh at her question and all three males, Roark, Brax and Trist, turned to look over their shoulders at us. We'd just transported to the planet and arrived at Natalie and Roark's home. Roark was leading my mates into the family room where I could hear Noah chattering away, probably telling his little sister they had guests.

Wow, all three of them together was a sight. Brawny and all alpha male goodness. I'd been envious of what Natalie had with Roark, but not any longer. I had *two* males who were all mine.

Natalie knew Brax well, but had not met Trist. And I

hadn't been able to talk to my best friend much since I'd been tested and transported to Battleship Zakar, and she'd been in the dark about everything I'd been through except the fact that I was matched to a Prillon.

I grinned. "Yes, he is big. *Everywhere.*"

She hugged me again then sighed, fanning herself. I started to follow the guys, but her hand on my arm stopped me. "You're happy?" Her gaze searched mine. "I know Brax was kind of jerk there for a while, but I don't think he meant to be one. In fact, I'd say it was just being your typical, clueless member of the male species."

I thought of Brax, of how far he'd come in such a short time. From being the "jerk" I'd left behind to the mate he was now. Committed. Ever present. Dominant.

I felt the weight of the chain that dangled between my breasts, the barely there tug it had on the nipple rings. I felt the medallions, warm and heavier against the skin of my upper belly. I wore loose tops now, for while some Trion mates liked to show off the fact they'd been claimed, Trist preferred to keep my...adornments...to himself. My fingers went to the collar about my neck, the outward sign of being his mate. Of being theirs. Trist was very possessive and didn't like to share with anyone but Brax. And while he wouldn't admit to Brax aloud that he loved the rings and chain, I could feel how it made him hot to gaze upon them. As for Brax, he'd gone from wanting to show me off to keeping me all to himself and Trist. Apparently, Trist had brought him around to the Prillon way of thinking.

Well, either that or the interested looks I was getting from the other warriors on the battleship. Trist assured me that not one would ever disrespect me, Lady Treval, and they hadn't. But that didn't mean the warriors did not admire Trist's mate.

A fact which drove Brax to distraction. The fact that I'd once thought him uninterested seemed like an alien concept now. Alien. I would have laughed at that, except I was now mated to two of them.

"He was being a dumb guy," I confirmed. "But he's proven himself to me, and to Trist, many times over."

In the family room, Roark was sprawled on the floor, propped up on one elbow, beside little Talia, who was lying on a pale green blanket. Noah was waving a toy so she could watch it. Her little legs kicked the air, clearly happy.

Trist sat in a chair, back straight, watching.

No, guarding me, more like. And I adored him for it.

Brax came over to me, wrapped an arm about my waist and kissed my forehead.

When Noah saw me, his little face lit up and he handed the toy to his father and ran over to me.

I dropped to my knees and wrapped his soft little body in a tight squeeze. "Hey, buddy! I think you grew a whole foot since I've seen you last."

He patted my cheek with his hand. "I did! Mommy said eating my vegbles makes me big."

"Don't tell your daddy, but if you keep it up, you'll be bigger than he is one day."

He leaned in, whispered in my ear, although it wasn't all that quiet. "Sooo much bigger."

Roark's head fell back and he laughed. Natalie scooped Noah up and gave him snuggle kisses, which made him giggle.

"I sense your need, mate," Brax whispered as I eyed my BFF with her son. I didn't envy her a mate any longer, but I did envy her children. Beautiful, sweet, precious children.

Even though I'd only been mated a short time, my ovaries had kicked into overdrive. Every time Trist's deep

voice commanded me to strip or every time Brax added the
extra chain that connected my nipple rings to a clamp on
my clit—bejeweled with a green gemstone, of course—I'd
craved not only their cocks, but the baby that could be
made.

That *had* been made.

I'd only just discovered I was pregnant before we transported off the battleship. It had been Brax himself who'd
given me my last birth control shot, but that had been weeks
and weeks ago, the last time we'd been together on Trion. It
had been over a month since the shot and when I'd been
tested. I hadn't even thought of it. Trist had never asked. To
be honest, I hadn't thought about children when Trist
claimed me. Then Brax appeared and threw my life into
chaos. Oh, I wanted children, always had, but never with a
ruthless intensity that meant *right now*, for before I was
mated, I hadn't considered it to be a real possibility.

But now it was much more than a possibility. With the
amount of sex we'd had, the amount of times they'd come
inside me, I was surely pregnant with triplets.

"I sense..." he began, then stilled. Growled. "*Gara.*"

Oh shit, the collars. I wasn't sure how Brax and Trist
would handle the announcement that we'd made a baby, for
we hadn't talked about it. We hadn't expected it. I had no
idea if they even really wanted one. I should have asked.
Maybe they didn't want children. Or maybe they did, but
not yet. Trist might freak. They had the Hive technology
they'd taken from the dead soldiers that attacked us, but the
Coalition was still trying to figure out how the stealth armor
was made. Reverse engineer the stuff. Figure out how to
detect it.

The battleship might not be safe for a baby. Was Trist
going to be upset? Angry that I hadn't asked them first? That

he would have a child to protect as well as a mate? Would Brax be dismayed that I hadn't remembered the birth control shot?

Oh, god. Did they even want a baby?

Trist popped up from his chair. "What is wrong, mate?"

He glanced around the room, instantly alert. His behavior was a signal to Roark that something was wrong and he scooped baby Talia up into his arms, jumping to his feet with a lithe grace I didn't expect. He made it across the room and had his arm about Natalie before I could blink.

"Holy crap, guys. Nothing's wrong," I said, reassuring them.

Roark didn't move from huddling his family close, but he'd handed the baby to Natalie and pulled out his weapon.

Trist crossed the room in three strides. "Something's wrong. I sense it. Fear. Panic."

I sighed all the way to my toes. This was *not* how I'd imagined breaking the news to them. I'd thought maybe candlelight and champagne and a sexy little green gown with slits everywhere...

"She's afraid to tell us she's pregnant," Brax said. I glanced up at him, saw the way the corner of his mouth was tipped up. Through the collar, I felt a swift jolt of relief that had my knees give out, but Brax wrapped an arm about me and held me close. I also felt satisfaction, happiness and even quite a bit of male pride.

I exhaled loudly, not realizing I'd held my breath.

"Mate," Trist growled, pulling me out of Brax's arms and into his. My face was smooshed into his chest and held so tightly I could barely move.

"Trist," I said. "I can't breathe."

Instantly, he pushed me away, looked me over as if *he* were the doctor. "Are you well? Sick? Feeling faint?"

I laughed then, finding a normally well-controlled Prillon completely flustered very funny.

"Ah, you laugh, mate," he said. "Just wait until your belly is round with child and you are waddling like... what is it on Earth?"

"A duck," I grumbled at the same time Natalie said, "She'll be a beached whale."

"You were, *gara*," Roark said to Natalie. "Twice. I think we should have another."

They began to bicker about who would carry their third child while Trist and Brax moved in so close I couldn't see Natalie or her family very well. "Guys, I'm fine."

"You are with child," Trist stated.

"She's not sick," Brax reminded. "Come sit down. You shouldn't be standing so much."

They led me to the couch and I rolled my eyes. "I can *stand* while pregnant."

"We must return to the battleship at once," Trist said, popping back up to his feet.

"I'm not having the baby for a little while yet. Probably eight months or more. We have time." I watched as he raked his hand through his light hair.

"I sense your amusement," he said, glaring at Brax. "How can I protect Miranda *and* a child?"

"She has two mates," Brax prompted, as if offended.

"That is of no help, Brax. When we have four children, we will be outnumbered. How will we cope, second?" Trist asked Brax. "We shall require a battle strategy."

Brax nodded. "We shall formulate a plan immediately upon our return to the Zakar."

I held up my hand. "Guys, you need to chill out. And what's this about *four* children? Four?"

Both men looked to me and grinned. "You enjoyed

making the first one," Brax said, waggling his eyebrows like Natalie often did.

I couldn't argue with that. "I'm not a brood mare. We'll see how this first one goes."

Both men frowned. "What is a brood mare? I sense it is not a good thing. As your mates, we will ensure you are never one," Trist said, Mr. Black and White.

"Then like I said, we'll see how the first one works out," I grumbled.

Trist went as white as a sheet, then looked to Brax. "Works out? Why shouldn't this baby *work out?* Brax, you must put her in a ReGen pod immediately. She needs to be scanned. Did you bring your medical equipment?"

Natalie laughed and Roark came over—all battle stations ready mode shut down—and slapped Trist on the back. "I've done this twice. The fear of something happening to your mate will ease the moment you see your baby. Then you'll panic about him... or her."

He was grinning. Trist was not. I bit my lip so as not to grin too much.

This was going to be so much fun, watching my two mates deal with me being pregnant, then having a baby. God, a baby!

I looked up at my men, all stoic and stuffy, calm and cool, and completely panicked.

Yes, they were mine. They were insane, but I wouldn't have it any other way.

A SPECIAL THANK YOU TO MY READERS...

Did you love Miranda, Brax and Trist? Want more? I've got *hidden* bonus content on my web site *exclusively* for those on my mailing list.

If you are already on my email list, you don't need to do a thing! Simply scroll to the bottom of my newsletter emails and click on the *super-secret* link.

Not a member? What are you waiting for? In addition to ALL of my bonus content (great new stuff will be added regularly) you will be the first to hear about my newest release the second it hits the stores—AND you will get a free book as a special welcome gift.

Sign up now! http://freescifiromance.com

LET'S TALK!

Interested in joining my not-so-secret Facebook Sci-Fi Squad? Share your testing match, meet new like-minded sci-fi romance fanatics!

JOIN Here:
https://www.facebook.com/groups/scifisquad/

Want to talk about the Cyborg's Secret Baby (or any Grace Goodwin book) with others? Join the SPOILER ROOM and spoil away! Your GG BFFs are waiting!

JOIN Here:
https://www.facebook.com/groups/ggspoilerroom/

FIND YOUR MATCH!

YOUR mate is out there. Take the test today and discover your perfect match. Are you ready for a sexy alien mate (or two)?

VOLUNTEER NOW!

interstellarbridesprogram.com

GET A FREE BOOK!

Join my mailing list to be the first to know of new releases, free books, special prices and other author giveaways.

http://freescifiromance.com

CONNECT WITH GRACE

Interested in joining my not-so-secret Facebook Sci-Fi Squad? Get excerpts, cover reveals and sneak peeks before anyone else. Be part of a closed Facebook group that shares pictures and fun news. JOIN Here: http://bit.ly/SciFiSquad

All of Grace's books can be read as sexy, stand-alone adventures. Her Happily-Ever-Afters are always free from cheating because she writes Alpha males, NOT Alphaholes. (You can figure that one out.) But be careful...she likes her heroes hot and her love scenes hotter. You have been warned...

www.gracegoodwin.com
gracegoodwinauthor@gmail.com

ABOUT GRACE

Grace Goodwin is a *USA Today* and international bestselling author of Sci-Fi & Paranormal romance. Grace believes all women should be treated like princesses, in the bedroom and out of it, and writes love stories where men know how to make their women feel pampered, protected and very well taken care of. Grace hates the snow, loves the mountains (yes, that's a problem) and wishes she could simply download the stories out of her head instead of being forced to type them out. Grace lives in the western US and is a full-time writer, an avid romance reader and an admitted caffeine addict.

ALSO BY GRACE GOODWIN

Mating Fever

Her Viken Mates

Fighting For Their Mate

Her Rogue Mates

Claimed By The Vikens

The Commanders' Mate

Interstellar Brides®: The Colony

Surrender to the Cyborgs

Mated to the Cyborgs

Cyborg Seduction

Her Cyborg Beast

Cyborg Fever

Rogue Cyborg

Cyborg's Secret Baby

Interstellar Brides®: The Virgins

The Alien's Mate

Claiming His Virgin

His Virgin Mate

His Virgin Bride

Other Books

Their Conquered Bride

Wild Wolf Claiming: A Howl's Romance

46504709R00114

Printed in Poland
by Amazon Fulfillment
Poland Sp. z o.o., Wrocław